Mall State

by Barak Avinoam

Book Cover design by yonatan avinoam

Photo cover credit: Jared Verdi on Unsplash

Photo cover credit: Victor Xok on Unsplash

Editor: Loren Milk

First paperback edition january 2022

2

This is a work of fiction.
Names, characters, places,
and incidents either are the
product of the author's
imagination or are used
fictitiously. Any
resemblance to
registeredcompanies/busin
esses, actual persons,
living or dead, events, or
locales is entirely
coincidental.

ISBN 978-965-599-888-7

Library of Congress Control Number: 2022900555

To Lilach

thank you for helping me step into the light

Chapter 1

Mazda moved away from the packaging company's gray buildings, to her eyes, white-marbled shops that were visible because of the bright sun rays that penetrated the large mall's dome. As she got closer to the border, she realized how small the packaging company was compared to the large mall that sheltered it. Guardians of the mall watched the young woman approach them, wearing a gray worker's jumpsuit. Even from a distance, looking at her body features put a smile on their faces. They did not imagine that the same woman with fragile walking and golden hair gliding over had been altered genetically. They noticed a woman's facial expression as of a human bee, a yellowish face with hairy black dots, even her hands were at the colour of a bee's skin with black dots.
" What are you looking at?", She asked with a tear in her eye. One guard answered: " We have already seen people like you, the bee group. "
Mazda replied: " I was born an ordinary person, but I was fed with food that improved me and made me more efficient and loyal ."
" If so, why do you want to go to the mall's section in which the food is completely normal? ", Asked another guard, while he extends his arm with the covered sleeve buttoned up to the shoulder. It surprised her to see his hologram shirt go awry and flashing as soon as he touched her, for the first time in

5

her life she saw a virtual garment covering so perfectly a human body. Mazda felt a twinge in her shoulder and the guard pulled his arm: " I injected you with the chip that gives you an Intranet connection of the mall, now you may enter." As she walked to the gate Mazda was blinded by the lights coming from the tall buildings that scraped up to the mall's dome, For minutes long stared at the bustle of shoppers around her from store to shop until her eyes focused on the train station.

Mazda sat on the train leading to the white palace where she hoped to meet her loved one, Sony with his slanting eyes and yellow hair, a bushy ancient admirably main marketer of the:" Democratic- companies Alliance's of the large shopping mall". thoughts ran through her mind about the moment she will meet him, she believed he was created for her and when they will meet they would NOT be able to separate, just as in the advertisement when Sony whispers to his beloved as she sleeps: " Let me smell your perfume and you'll get my touch of guilt ". The train to the far north quickly flew at ultrasonic speed, approaching the north division. In the train cart an announcer call: " We are passing over the Mediterranean." The view of a sparkling sea appeared through the window, Mazda tries to ignore the other passengers who stared at her strange skin color brightened by the minute. She connected the intranet through the chip and watched the information in her mind. She began to read: "The mall's glass sutured after connecting the five continents' marine trenches, to save electricity illumination light directed toward the mall's glass walls on the ground. "companies Alliance" led to world peace and brought the purest water." Suddenly, a music advertisement interrupted the text: " In honor of a century of peace we are pleased to introduce the first "feelings-reader", only 200 Euler and it is yours. Read the feelings of the person closest to you

And may he live with you forever, soon available in the Northern general department store." Mazda said to herself: " Exactly where I'm going, I have to get it. Maybe this way I can make Sony love me the way I love him." Mazda connected to the intranet again using the chip that runs in her blood and found a link to the White Palace "The Northern Palace is located on the large shopping mall, in fact, it is the first branch of the mall that extends its boundaries to connect to the western mall that was called the United States. Georgeo, the big entrepreneur, connected the two malls through miles of glass tubes stretching between the continents of Europe and America. City-dwellers migrated to the air-conditioned mall due to extreme global warming, looking for a cool and airy place to live in. A hundred years ahead, The big mall has become a great consumer nation. The terms to be accepted as a consumer to the mall was to leave any sign of ethnic, religious, and national identity outside it, The loyalty to Georgeo's brand is the only religion permitted. " An announcement was heard on the train: " We have arrived at the last stop, passengers are asked to get off the carts." Mazda quickly got off the exit before the rest of the passengers blocked her passage. She noticed that the mall's walls were light blue and not sunlight colored, as in the mall's high area. " I am close to the White Palace ", she thought in her heart when she walks step by step to the exit when her rucksack was on her back. Human-like robots at the height of children with flashing heads in red offered her some of the mall's brands, Mazda recognized the brands she had seen when she came out of the packaging company gates. A robot projected a hologram of the dress she longed for, all Mazda could think about was the moment in which she will meet the object of her love. Her belly cried out of hunger, the mall's air-conditioned smelled of intoxicating spring blossoms, which intensified the feeling of hunger. Mazda step closer to the nearest restaurant in the mall: "Georgeo's", an automatic door opened, and she walked in and sat down on a chair leaning against the shop window, instantly a service robot approached her and opened four options blinking on the screen on his stomach. The screen was divided into four equal squares. On the top right was a picture of a juicy steak with the caption:" a complete protein ", to the left the was a picture of a loaf of bread that says: " carbohydrate-energy ", Mazda looked at the bottom left of the screen that appeared in the image of white cream that said: " Sweet vegetable fat. " The lower right side was a picture of colorful pills with the caption: " The three major food groups in a variety of flavors". Mazda looked at the list of flavors that were unknown to her because she arrived from the packaging company and consumed genetically modified foods designed to preserve the genetic structure of the body and was tasteless. She chose the " The three main food groups " pill. She pressed her finger to the robot's eye for identification, out of the robot's long tongue which came out of the robot's mouth sat a colored pill. After swallowing the pill, Mazda saw another pill carried on the robot's tongue moving toward her. After taking the pill, a pill stretched to her again, and so on. Mazda tried to stay away from the robot and left the restaurant. one robot has blocked the entrance with his body disallowing her to leave. Mazda ran towards the entrance of the kitchen: " Is it a malfunction or did I win some the lottery?" There she was stopped by an old lady: " Girl, if the robot bothers you, you can simply move your finger again. The robot thinks you're still hungry, he can't read thoughts." Mazda responded to her when the robot is standing behind her with his tongue out: " I am not familiar with this custom, usually I get what I ask ".

The old lady replied with humiliated eyes: " This is not the case, girl, you must consume food until the robot discovers that you are full according to your blood readings. "

Mazda tapped her finger on the robot's eye and it did not respond and continued to hold his tongue in front of her when a pill lay on it.

" I will have to disable it, I hope I won't get jailed for this..."

Mazda got angry,

The old woman replied immediately: " No, do not stop it by force. He will report to the central computer. I have an idea, come with me quickly down the stairs. The robot can not get up the stairs because he is a hoover with no legs. "he Mazda followed the lady up the stairs, and immediately, an automatic door closed behind them. Mazda wandered around the dim room in which glowing jars of various colors stood. Mazda approached one of the jars on the shelf and saw an animal's body float, curled into itself. The animal seemed unfamiliar to her. " This is 30 weeks old horse's embryo," said the old lady to Mazda: " From a young age I was carefully collecting samples of the fetus of animals that have not yet been born, a collection of creatures who do not live in the big mall but once lived outside. ' Enthusiastically, Mazda continued to walk around the room. The old woman looked at Mazda and pulled her hand into the jar with a small collection of insects: " Do you recognize what's in that jar?", Mazda opened her mouth: these bees, they have my dotted yellow complexion, its the first time I see the original creatures to which I was fitted to. "

The old woman replied: " You are human, just like me, but you have part of these little creatures inside you, if you continue to consume food that is not genetically changed you will become an ordinary woman. "

Mazda replied: " I feel normal right now. " Mazda felt something unnatural about her and looked down. " What is

10

this smell? " asked Mazda, amazed, looking around for the source of the smell.

" Just eat my dear, " the old lady took a giant spoon, went to the pot underneath the fire, and filled a tablespoon with substance not identified, and poured it into a bowl.

Mazda said: " I don't know how to eat it. "

" Just put it in your mouth," said the old woman. Mazda tried to hold the slippery substance between her lips, but it slipped and only a small portion went into her mouth, a big smile smeared on her face while feeling the salty spicy, and hot texture of the stew. " It's a taste I've never felt before, " Mazda said.

" My name is Materna ," the woman replied with a cheeky smile on her face, " I knew this smile of mine would be followed by yours as well, there is nothing more satisfying than the pleasure of others enjoying the creation of your making that touched there heart. I would not ask you what is missing in my dish because of your inexperience, you cannot say. "

" How did you learn to do such amazing things? My body never felt like this, this feeling starts from the mouth and down to the throat and continues." Suddenly, Mazda held her shrunken stomach and wanted to move to the window, and vomited off the window from the second floor of the building.

11

" My child, I must not have let you put so much meat into your stomach. God knows how degenerate it was since your birth."

" All I've become accustomed to is transgenic and tasteless food. Why don't you offer your wares at one of the stores?" Mazda asked in amazement as she lightly wiped her mouth with a cloth Materna gave her.

" Do not be a silly child, The ones who decide what would be sold reside in the White Palace. No one would listen to an old woman like me. See also what damage my dish has caused you, I am usually sipping it in small sips and slowly for about an hour or so."

" I'd be happy if you teach me how to cook like this, we should sell it on the street in tiny dishes, we can charge about a half Euler per serving ". Mazda saw how her human qualities of passion and creativity are overcoming her Bee features.

" Do not be silly, my lovely girl, we should not engage in peddling, it's against the law, the mall's police would catch you in an hour. You know what? I'll teach you how to cook, and in return, you will run the local restaurant branch, I will oversee the robots and the supply of pills.

Mazda embraces Materna: " Thank you. I would love to learn from you how to cook, it will be the best inheritance I've ever received ".

Materna winked to Mazda: " Don't eulogize me yet, I plan to be here for a long time. "

"Where can I sleep?" Mazda asked her.
" You can settle on the roof beneath the mall transparent dome, but first I want to show you something that has been in my family for generations. Mazda and Materna entered a small elevator shaft which was located behind a red curtain on the second floor. Mazda saw how the elevator brings them within seconds, above them shimmering the Dome of the mall. " look round, " Materna whispered in her ear, in front of Mazda revealed a green sight, trails of crops on one side and a wet rice paddy on the other, in the mud trudging pink pigs and cackling hens. Mazda lay on the soft and warm field And closed her eyes with her hands spread to the sides.

Chapter 2

The hovercraft cruised in an exemplary fashion over the tall white palace buildings. While they float they try not to exceed the height of the middle of the glowing buildings, underneath them lays the plastic green gardens and fountains. Georgeo sat alone in the back of the middle car of the convoy, looking down into groups of people. The first car in the convoy stopped in front of a white wall, suddenly the wall was split into a square that began to rise from the bottom, a black hole opened, and the caravan entered into the main tower. Georgeo felt the darkness descending upon him, his face winced as he asked the computer of the vehicle to turn on the interior light. After a few seconds as the vehicle chair has raised, the car roof opens and he finds himself back on stage inside his leisure room, sitting, while a bunch of robot servants waiting for his command. They were arranged in a circle around a small stage that was about two times larger than his belly and spanned the chair.

" Gogol, do you hear me?" Read Georgeo through its internal chip.

" I listen, Your Majesty, " Gogol replied.

" Stop scribbling on the net, you idiot, I told you without exciting nicknames before Two o'clock in the afternoon.

Come here for a relaxed meeting for just the two of us, dinner

14

as usual at my expense. " Said Georgeo, while his shaggy
mustache was slightly swaying.

Within a minute, Gogol walked quickly into Georgio's sun-
drenched room with his head covered and his body wrapped
in a green robe that reached to his feet. "I told you to come
here in a minute." He shouted at Gogol standing in front of
him.

"You said and I did. Maybe I was a few seconds late. I'm
sorry sir."

"There is no time to procrastinate. I was notified of the
packaging company at the south." Georgio said to him
vigorously as he turned his face away from him at the view in
the window.

Gogol read the text on the small screen he held in his two
clasped hands: "There seems to have been a decline in their
ability to supply us with raw materials since the fire we
caused last month."

"Great, I'll make sure to send nanobots to find their way out
of the mall from where they import the raw materials,"
Georgio answered him with a grin on his crumpled, plump
face.

"And for the next issue, what about lowering wages for sales employees? They will be given a caffeine pill gift at the expense of cutting salaries."

Gogol interrupted: "It requires a huge campaign that will cost us a lot."

"Not anymore, don't forget the copy-writing software that will cut costs. As for the graphics, we have fixed templates that work for a hundred years and we won't have to hire the former designers again." Suddenly, a flash appeared in the right window of the rounded room, from which sprang from a pink background on which was broadcast by Heinze, the palace's main chambermaid. She looked scared: "Sir, your child, Disney, refuses to study with his teacher, he was playing with the new doll you brought him again."

"I don't have time for this Heinze. From my point of view, take the doll and hand it to some beggar on the street."

She replied: "It reminds me that a beggar chased me down to the palace gate, why shouldn't the boy hand out the doll and help the beggars?"

"Sorry ma'am," Georgio snapped angrily: "You have been given the most important role in the palace – to watch my child, not to get yourself dirty in the dusty street. As for beggars, it is known that this is their livelihood, they also have a role in the huge economy I conduct. When a beggar on the street looks at you, he looks bleak, his head slumped and hand outstretched. He works on your conscience. As soon as you give him money, he will sell you the happiness and mental satisfaction you received from helping him. That's his contribution to the world. " Georgio continued his speech without taking a breath: "As the person who has sold to the largest amount of people, I am the man who has helped the most and has made the most money ever since. I am the biggest donor to humanity since time immemorial because most people have chosen to buy from me and spend the Their money on my products. "

"Let me interrupt you both," said Gogol, "but there is your medical interest."

"Yes I see, wait for a second Gogol."

"Do you understand what I told you, Heinze?" He turned to Georgio calmly after relaxing from the speech he plunged into her: "Yes, sir, I will submit myself to deliver the doll to Disney." The call broke off, the screen disappeared and the sunlight swept through the room on the right.

"If you're going to talk to me about the frozen organs, we'll have to do it discreetly." Georgio whispered to him, and

Gogol left the room: "Sir, I have to go back to my wife. I have some arrangements in the family. Sorry to miss our meal together."

"Just don't forget your important visit to the packaging company," Georgio yelled at him as Gogol walked away from him: "Don't worry sir, it will be done."

Disney, the bright-haired baby cried incessantly as he sat in a gold-plated coop. Flashing lights around him, robotic arms croaking around him, one of the arms holding a gold pacifier with powder pads polluting with scented materials on his forehead, all of which the therapist winced with non-stop chirping commands, she used to take a short breath every minute and a half as she stood and watched him sitting on his scarlet pillow and crying most of the time.

Georgio came in his hovering chair trying to get off, but he rushed forward to grab hold of his heavy body and put both feet on the luxurious wall-to-wall carpet that stretched across the darkroom.

"Let me carry it in my hands, hope you cook him a fine chicken broth," Georgio said as Hinze hears and pauses as he walks over to his son and ignores her, reaches for his son, raises it for two seconds, puts it on the pillow and, again, Whenever his hands grew tired, he regained some strength and returned to lift his son in the air until his hands were tired again. A thin smile popped over Georgio's face, he was dazzled by the crying baby's sparkling slippery head. Suddenly, a red screen opened in the room on which the scientist-advisor, Intelan, face lay.

"Sir, do you hear me?"As usual, Intelan performed a device test because he was always afraid that the inter-communication between him and Georgio would not work. This question always irritated Georgio who was busy at that moment with his son across the simulated hologram screen.

"Intelan, you're bothering me right now..." Georgio replied, still smiling at his baby's angel face while admiring his bullet nose: "We've reached a breakthrough with the new 'Emotional Readers' you have invited." Intelan told him as he made a quotation mark with his fingers as he continued to rotate and examine the communication system he had won at that moment.

"The order is still valid and I expect to see their demo on the three types of people: palace resident, a mall citizen, and packaging company employee," Georgio said.

"Yes sir, Gogol said he would get us the third type soon, probably a senior character who will be doing a demo before we can start the experiment."

"Excellent Intelan, I am happy for any progress on the emotion readers," Georgio replied with the same codeword used by Intelan. The red screen closed, Georgio let Hinze continue her work as he left the room in his hovering armchair.

Chapter 3

Long lines extended from the doors of the "Georgio's" store out to the mall's corridors. At the beginning of the line, Mazda was operating the order booth control panel, managing the robots: one was cleaning food boxes and handkerchiefs from the floor and tables, the other serving pills to the diners. A Robot waiter took orders from mall consumers who stood in the line and from palace workers who stood in the shorter line.

Mazda watched the orders screen filled with inquiries and complaints from consumers about poor service. In her mind, she saw a list of referrals smeared on the screen rising like a river overflowing from the device's holes and down to the floor. She woke up and remembered that she had to worry about the robots asking her questions too. Thus eleven hours have passed since Mazda woke up with leg pain when the food pill she had eaten hours ago had already been digested, leading to stomach cravings announcing dinner time. But at "Georgio's" restaurant, her work has not yet been completed.

The last customer left the shop, Mazda fell asleep on the counter with a smile on her face, Sonny has been revealed to her, smiling as she woke, gunk in her eyes. Sony reaches for her and leads her to the filming scene, cameras from all sides, she is wearing makeup of pink and gold on her face, wrapped in a gold and silver metallic garment. Behind the red curtain, Sony emerges with a shimmering purple cloak, cheering the audience that cheers him back and she is now on stage with him. Sonny walks over to her, his blonde hair shining in the stage lights, coming up to her and about to kiss her with his lips, she tells him: "I can't believe it, it's like a dream," and then she wakes up on the counter again. A new day has dawned at the great mall.

On the walls of the mall's white marble corridors in yellow artificial lighting, the turrets of circular, hexagonal, and rectangular stores appear as they walk around mesmerizing holograms with mesmerizing perfection of appearance and in-store consumers buy and fade to see their merchandise. Amid the rioting in these corridors, Mazda is determined to enter the White Palace. In her account, all the money she saved in her job at the food store. she is being pushed among the people who are still longing for more, she's eager to live her dream today, to meet Sonny who is only a few miles apart.

She reached one of the white wall gates that separated her from the white palace which was a city of its own, on the wall flashed screens with publicity broadcasts including mirror images of hackers' attempts to hack into the wall to attract the attention of the guards. Presenters who presented various products that were the priests of this consumerist religion featured the commercial holograms. Next to the gate, which was as a black-brown checkerboard that occasionally opened for flying vehicles, to get in and out, Mazda stood admiring the size and intensity of the gate, smiling in ecstasy.

In her attempts to enter through the gate, two broad-shouldered guards stood in front of her: "Ma'am, did you pay the entrance fee?"

"No, I haven't paid yet. I didn't know you had to pay, I have thirty-one eullars in my account, hope this is enough."

The guard looked at Mazda with a mocking look on his face: "Try to pay at the computer on your left, but I think you need at least a hundred, where can a simple girl like you get so much money?" The guard asked suspiciously as he looked at her face up from above.

She replied, "You see, I came from the packing company in the south, where it's easier to save, but the prices are higher for those who crave merchandise from the mall outside. Let's just say I inherited it from my family who perished."

The guards who heard this were amazed at her words and one of them laughed cynically while the other answered Mazda: "I don't think you understand, you innocent girl. The entrance for a hundred eullars is for tourists only and not for the sake of residence that is for the palace staff only. Enter a tour of the palace. In any case, you don't have to try. "The other guard burst into his words: "Sure enough when you're a foreigner and came from the rebellious packaging company." Mazda realized that her chances of getting in were slim, she was thinking hard for a solution under the pressure exerted by the guards. Feeling she had to leave and trying to get that one hundred Eular, she turned her delicate little body against the strength and height of the guards and made her way back to Georgio's store branch where she knew she could spend the next night.

The lights in the non-air-conditioned part of the mall began to darken as Mazda walked along the wall, hoping it might break out. Mazda focused her gaze on a flickering advertisement for an energy drink, the screening focused on a white spot on the wall. The same white spot cut off from the wall and fell to the floor about 100 yards from where Mazda was standing. From the white spot, a hologram in the shape of a humanoid robot appeared next to her. This was the image of the newly promoted advertising presenter on the wall. A woman of about forty, wearing a pink, swollen dress with a stylized oval-pink feather cap, approached the hologram. It was obvious to Mazda that all she wore was a hologram projected onto her white suit, like most mall women and some men have, but it was a convincing and pretty projection for what made Mazda smile enviously. The colored-dress woman seemed to talk to the hologram figure, bowing to him and handing him what appeared to be some invoice notes. The robot in return put his hand over the woman's head and shed a pale white light over her by saying, "Bless you woman, thanks to your donation, I received a sign from God that Georgio is its only prophet and his teachings are truth teachings. Let us praise Georgio and buy his expensive goods. "

The crowd that gathered around the woman and the robot sang in the chorus: "Let us congratulate Georgio and buy his expensive goods."The sight reminded her of the history lessons she learned during a time when she was a student in the packaging company's nursery. She learned there about the time of churches and mosques that spread their teachings around the world in a missionary way and donated their best money to the church. "Excited by the experiences of the day, she went back to sleeping in the sleeping capsule bedroom near the store.

Chapter 4

Gogol entered the packaging company's Hive, called by the Companies Register: "The Southern Carton and Raw Materials Company." He was taken by two guards to the Queen of the Hive, before embarking on a meeting with her, he read the Inner-network about a comprehensive study written on her: "Subara - the original name of the company manager, management based on biological theory and beehive studies in which everyone collaborates for the survival of The group, where she was stationed as the queen. The difference between this company and a regular cooperative is in consuming a reversible repair gene that is given to all employees of the company, including the queen. The expression of the gene results in unique traits that have the characteristic of bees. "Gogol continued to carefully read the appendix of the entry: "In recent years, the packaging company has begun experiments on training hybrid animals from other animals than bee's to expand their scope and efficiency." Gogol came prepared in advance with a neutralizing drug, which he would submit to Subara, presented as a gift along with the "helmet of emotion" trade offer. Gogol thought as he was led into the Queen's room: "Of course, she will refuse out of fear of being emotionally manipulated, but the drug that we will be brought to her without her noticing will cause her to lose her loyalty to the group and allow us to find the path outside the packaging company and take control of her as Georgio's wishes. " There was no room for verbal and aesthetic expression in a society whose sole purpose is survival against the large mall that contained it. Gogol felt the power of being more representative and not obedient. For the first time in his life, he calls the shots, the bottleneck that directs the flow from his master to a completely external place. But on the other hand, he felt some fear of his master, "maybe he was looking at me? Maybe he oversees me? Maybe he will get angry if the result is not exactly as he expected?" So he tried to elevate his confidence in the face of the Queen. Gogol was led into a control center with indicator lights, a woman sat and fiddled with touch screens and buttons as she typed a lot of input into them that prevented her from paying attention to his entrance with the guards. "We brought the messenger, madam," said the guard standing on Gogol's right side. The Queen looked up from the shimmering screens and lights, looked at Gogol, and said with worried eyes, "Hello, welcome, sit back and tell me why they sent you?"

Gogol was surprised at the sight that was revealed to him, after all, the queen sat in front of him as a clerk doing her job instead of sitting on a royal throne, lowering orders to her subjects as in the old legends. Gogol opened with his speech dictated by Georgio: "I was sent here to offer you the best technology and produce from the mall's company. I am sure we can do business beyond supplying raw materials for cash. We have elaborate means that the government cannot sell to you".

The queen interrupted Gogol's statement, saying, "I have to protect the interests of the company employees, I can't get any favors if that's what you mean. I don't think there is a reason for a competing company like us to trade with your company beyond what we are obligated to in the "mall's state "constitution.

Gogol looked down and answered her with a lecture: "We already know your policy, but I have provided a radiation reader of gamma rays that can ensure the safety of miners and robotic loggers so that they do not transfer the radiation to the mall. My Queen, here you go, for reading emotions, a revolutionary instrument, with its help you can check every attempt of rebellion and strive among your employees.

Subara immediately shook her head, she replied: "I've already told you I can't get favors for myself, something in me refuses to do so. Certainly it's because I was born with the "hive management" gene that made me get this job."Gogol paused and said enthusiastically, "My dear queen, you are doing this for the safety of the group. Think of it as a safeguard for your management efficiency, you get no pleasure in penetrating the intimate thoughts of others, You were not born with the ability of self-indulgence that contradicts the group's interest, do you? ".

Subara took the device, looked at his bluish glow, and said, "I'll think about it, but first come and do the formal tour in the company's departments."

Gogol smiled lightly, thinking he was close to his goal of convincing the queen, and that the device would be a double-edged sword.

Subara and Gogol accompanied by two security guards began to tour the corridors of the company, from the aisles of the accounting department to the materials processing department and the computer department. Gogol was not interested in the scholarly explanations of the queen, what caught his eye was precisely the warm and pleasant relationships of the employees with one another, without any sense of status or requirement of obedience, each doing his job with joy and satisfaction as dictated by the genes added to his body It is clear that he will receive an equal share of the company's profits. All of these actions were done in the fullest acquaintance of all the hundreds of company employees intimately. These relationships seem to be pouring in from all sides like the radioactive light coming out of the mall's glass roof each morning, this atmosphere has inspired a bright and warm feeling as you open your eyes and notice that a new day begins. Gogol felt that he had arrived at the happy and Non-alienated collective that exists beyond the relationship between a man and a woman and their children. Let alone in the corridors of the enslaved mall. Even his relationship with his wife would not compare to what he saw in his eyes here that day, and certainly not to the utilitarian friendships he had experienced with his working colleagues around Georgio, his master.

The tour ended again in Subara's room and she turned to Gogol: "After thinking and consulting with our team of scientists, I decided to try using the device on you, wouldn't you mind me reading your feelings?"

Gogol, who was ready in time for a polite bow request, answered the queen: "No problem, you are invited to direct and turn on the device. When the device changes color from bluish to red, you will gradually feel my feelings."Gogol rose from his bow and shook hands, waiting for her to begin. Subara immediately sensed Gogol's long-suffering feelings and delays following the tour, unaware of the drug injected into her blood. While admiring her open eyes from the emotional presentation, Gogol noticed how the drug is spreading in her body and affecting its genetic composition and transforming it into a "normal human mutation," that's how the packaging company employees called the mall's people."My Queen, we will be in touch with you soon, I am sure we will be happy to cooperate and that you will love our suggestions."Gogol shouted as he turned his back to her as he was led by the guards outside the company gates.

Chapter 5

A team of five police officers walked through the hall of the mall stores and made their way between shoppers and White Palace workers who were crowded in the stores that Sunday.

"The courier who sold everything for only a eular has already been arrested?"The commander exclaimed in his tiny chip as the four policemen under his command lurked behind him.

The voice from the other side exclaimed: "He has arrived and will be put into the main dungeon in the cellars of the White Palace."The connection broke off, the commander stopped and looked at the "Georgio's" branch to his right. He picked up his black goggles that were attached to his black helmet and looked toward the crowded entrance of shoppers waiting at the storefront door. The police squad worked the commander's way through the queue of those who kept their eullar for their only meal that day, some of whom were white palace workers hurrying from a chore to chanting a pill for quick gratification.

Everyone without exception has moved obediently away, no one wants to lose his job by disobeying the mall's police. Materna immediately approached the policeman identifying him by the shape of his hat and his serious facial expression.

32

It was impossible not to think that he was the commander of the crew.

"How can I help you?" Materna formally addressed him, as she learn to do over the years.

The commander replied: "Are you unaware that this place was supposed to be closed a month ago? We did not receive a request of approval from the main computer, we came to check if a hostile takeover or malfunction of the communication systems occurred."The cops around him looked at the starving crowd waiting to be fed. It seemed strange to them to perform an "aggressive closing process" as described in the protocol while the place has a vital role to play in a hungry environment. At that time Materna and the commander discussed between them the burcaucratic processes of holding the store that was wholly owned by the White Palace. Mazda made sure to hide behind the counter as the service robots moved just about an inch above the magnetic metal paved ground, shining white and charging them with electricity. "There is no doubt that the plug will be pulled immediately and they will become a silent pile of plastic with no use," Mazda thought to herself while trying to hear the conversation through the crowd. Materna and the cops came out after half an hour of thunderous conversation, only Mazda could hear the call because the doors were already locked. Materna knew that Mazda was hiding there, and implored the cops that she had to take her personal belongings before leaving for the last time: "Georgio and the big mall are everything, you know the scriptures?"The commander asked. Materna pleaded that she was just taking an old chip from the era that the chips were outside of the human body where her memories are stored. She went up to the attic with the police following her, Materna opened the door to allow Mazda in the order they will escape, Mazda fled. Mazda ran inside the crowd as if there was an unconscious connection between her and this old Materna, which she felt as if she is the queen of the hive. The genetic influence has already expired. It may have been a maternal memory that came to her, something more rooted that made her feel a deep connection, the nuclear family unit she had lost and was not supposed to feel like that as a member of the Packaging company. For the first time in her life, she felt the pain of the loss of Materna as she never had felt about her family who perished in the fire. For some reason, she couldn't remember the details about her family while living in the packaging company. Mazda felt tired and completely confounded, she knew that her only way to sleep tonight would be only in a capsule managed freely in exchange for viewing some commercials. There was no other option for the consumers of the mall, except that they were happy to watch advertisements that were strange to Mazda, advertisements that were, in their view, an oracle provided by Georgio: "If you bought a product that has earned you everything, you have done a mitzvah!" Mazda had trouble keeping her eyes open while watching the video projected two inches from her face. The capsule was slightly larger than an average human body but warm. Every other resident of the mall was happy to watch the commercials and sleep while feeling satisfied by the staff he did, but Mazda felt uncomfortable and had trouble falling asleep, she was preoccupied, what would be her fate, how would she save money for entering the White Palace and what would be the fate of Materna be? Sony appeared in an advertisement for a perfume, his eyes spoke to her exclusively, now another Indecision was added to her head, whether to purchase the perfume as a reminder of Sony on her body or to save it for the entrance to the palace?

In the morning Mazda woke up feeling no longer bound to the forces that held her in the packaging company, her stomach juices shaking, she felt a strong need to initiate something and take her fate in her hands. She realized by herself that the change was the result of the loss of desire-regulating gene activity, a passion that she was beginning to feel for Sony and intensified as she consumed non-engineered food. She had to buy and conquer, transcend the dullness of the other residents of the mall in a unique and grandiose look. Passion-regulated genes are the ones that induce altruistic behavior in humans. As a means of backing up, the packaging companies give all its residents and in addition to the queen a daily dose of pellets inserted into food, which the packaging company residents consciously consume to avoid the forbidden and repugnant feelings of desire and desire to take control of others. This creature helped the human race survive under harsh conditions, as small flocks, but was a burden on large organizations dominated by a powerful alpha male. Mazda was aware of the sin of that feeling but had no means to resist. In addition, she thought it would be good to connect with these feelings in order to achieve her new purpose that gave special meaning to her life, now that her family is gone. She saw nothing wrong with finding love. The first step Mazda has taken was to go back to the store, or rather to the store that was closed by the mall's management. "I hope they didn't confiscate all the plants and animals on the roof of the building," she thought to herself. The store was indeed closed when it reached the two-story building. She saw that it was possible to climb to the roof without risk of physical injury, as the walls of the building were rough in a way that allowed people to climb on them in case of a robot malfunction. To her delight, Mazda discovered the wheat fields that were planted at a depth of 4 feet of shovelful put there by Materna during her long life, it was a delusional spectacle to see a planting field, fruit trees, chickens, and goat yielding milk on the mall's roof. All she had to do was prepare and sell stews, without the computerized and reported arrangement to the mall manager who requires a Georgio - approved operating license. Because Mazda sought to earn the amount of a hundred eullars, even a loan can not be taken at the mall other than a universal subsistence salary. This salary was given to all residents of the mall state and the sum that did not exceed a few eullars.

Mazda was accustomed to making crates made by her bare hands since childhood, the raw materials were the lunchbox wrappers that were reminiscent of the traditional sandwiches and burgers the company packed a century ago and today are meant to be a huge pack containing feeding pills and 90% air.

In the boxes, Mazda hid the loot of grains, vegetables, and eggs she had taken from the attic, she had no way of knowing how to slaughter the chickens and goats and therefore gave up the dubious pleasure. She thought demand would outstrip supply, as she had learned in history lessons, she made a considerable effort to recall her humble and affable teacher mumbling stories and legends about the pre - ecological disaster. At a time when everyone is exposed to the open air with a few fields and lots of small palaces for each family, more than the family room that the packaging company employees had and more than the bedroom rental room they had to sleep in her last few nights there. In that old world, people would get their bread if not from work then in commerce, an operation where they receive money for goods. The survival instinct, combined with her knowledge, directed her to the streets, where the demand of the hungry masses for goods would already reach her and once she had the advantage, even temporary, over the mall's unlimited power, she could see the profit. The only thing that deterred her was the fear of being caught, she stood with the piles of crates in the middle of the mall corridors and waited.

For several days Mazda's venture was a huge success, dozens of curious people who stood for the first few hours and did not understand the meaning of these scents that cause them gastric ulcers, huddled in a large queue behind the piles of boxes Mazda loaded with mini goodies, cooking and raw food. She learned to make stews according to Matrana's recipes, vegetable pies, wheat berries, and other baked goods. It was the second time in history that man discovered the wheat, in a mall selling simulated hologram-clad details projected from computer chips. Private details that their appearance would change on a gray suit. These products were visioned in the minds of dozens of engineers and artists in the White Palace and marketed in mall stores as cult accessories that must be purchased to win Georgio's heavenly recognition. For the first time, the residents of the mall met with consumer products that could be inserted into the body, which are not nutritional pills of synthesized foods, but real foods.

38

Sunan and Fox, average reporters who left the White Palace for the "News of the Purchase" magazine each morning in order to survey new products that appear and are screened throughout the mall. They did not expect to see the long line of customers from the store, did not mention in their plan a queue at the end of which stands a girl with crates.

"We should give up all of our plans, it is redundant to re-examine hologram clothing from ancient times when new and different news can be brought, "Fox told Sunan.

Looking at Mazda and the long queue till its end, she replied: "Do you know that consuming physical goods that did not come out of the palace in Georgio's spiritual teaching is forbidden? All that is allowed is pure, visual, or literal information. We must not expose the public to anything that encourages breaking the palace's exclusivity, "Sunan said in such a succession that nearly engulfed her soul with dense speech, the curiosity that led her to a major journalist position was the one that immorally pushed her toward the gathering. Fox followed Sunan as he always did, he quit his career as the host of the main news edition only to be beside her on the streets. Even as she moved toward the food stall, he followed her regardless of the situation, in fact, he could say that he had ended his job as a reporter and devoted his time to be with her out of his obsession with her. All that matters is to be beside her and much less be a reporter. So it turned out that Sunan and Fox stood at the beginning of the queue as befits for palace workers, with no urgency, shouts, and raised eyebrows from the audience but with astonishment and excitement. This is a response the reporters have become accustomed to from mall consumers who have already seen people of careers devoting their time for work and not just for ritual consumption.

Sunan casts questions on Mazda: "Where did you come from? Where did you get all these resources? What pushed you to initiate?" Mazda realized she had been exposed and came up with an idea to take the 147eulars at the wallet in the chip inside her body, abandon the goods and flee to the area before being reported to high ranks that will alert the police. To the amazement of Fox and Sunan, Mazda ran back toward the entrance of the palace, leaving her wares behind, while amazed at her sudden disappearance, Sunan urged Fox to pursue the girl interviewed for less than a minute.

Fox grabbed Sunan's shoulder, turned her facing him, and said, "Let's take a photo and report on the products here. It looks like the food served to people about a century ago, before the dome was closed upon the world."

Sunan looked away from him as soon as he finished talking, turning her back to Fox as he followed her rummaging through the crates. "Right, we have enough material here for a whole week's articles for the White Palace Magazine viewers. It is worthwhile interviewing shoppers who are lining up for that mysterious lady and how they were impressed with her surprising entrepreneurial spirit," she replied back to Fox as he approached one of the people at the beginning of the queue. The line began to disperse when one of the men was flooded with a bright white coat hologram, asking Fox: "Are you going to take the boxes or can we pry them?" Fox took him aside and asked him questions, while more and more people were scattered everywhere, disappointed with the sale event that was nipped in the bud.

Chapter 6

On the highest floor of the octagonal tower in the White Palace, Gogol looked out the window of his penthouse apartment for five minutes before taking the ferry to the prime minister's house on the north side of the mall. A government that allegedly controlled the entire mall state population. Prime Minister Peugeot knew about this meeting of the mall's actual ruler, who is Georgio, and waited impatiently for him to attend this meeting as if it were the most fateful day of his life. "Adoba, I'm leaving for one night, Georgio sent me."

Gogol's wife was very angry that her husband was leaving her and replied: "I have long expected you to stop those disappearances, ask Georgio to let you be a simple clerk. I am just not willing to stay with a husband who does not devote his time to me, I want us to be together and take time to set up Our family. You're not a slave to anyone, you don't understand that Georgio is just taking advantage of your talent, you're not earning anything from it. "

Gogol quickly answered her as he looked out the window: "It seems to me that you just want me to be your slave, a pet who does chores for you. I'm tired of bringing you money, tidying up your household affairs, and bringing children into the world."

Adoba was shocked to hear his words, bowed her head, and said: "I really love you Gogol, too bad you don't even believe your wife. Your fear of Georgio blinds you to a situation you can't trust me?!". At the most inappropriate moment, Georgio beeped through Gogol's chip, he answer out of fear, which further angered Adoba. With fury, she impulsively ran to the bedroom with the door closed behind her. Gogol was slightly confused, he answered Georgio as he reluctantly advanced toward the ferry that was waiting for him on the roof of the tower.

Peugeot, The premier of the Mall, is named after an ancient automobile company founded in the 19th century, because he was born the first of ten brothers, just like the first automobile company in history. He was ambitious at birth, after a week of crawling on the floor, which saved him from spending his first days on the public incubator. As a kid, he even wanted to serve in the White Palace, even though he was born to a consumer family from the mall. At the age of eleven, he joined the ruling party: the "Consumer Party" aimed at protecting Georgio's consumers from exposure to other entrepreneurial brands that could set up competing companies. Through this party that has always won 100 percent of the electorate, Peugeot thought he would qualify for the prime minister's role in giving him a foothold in the White Palace one day. To this day, he did not know how, but he was confident that with the right relationships with those close to Georgio he would one day succeed in getting there and serving the great Georgio himself. One of the ways in which he succeeded was the formulation of fairly populist laws known as the "Restricting Companies Act" which prevented the establishment of competing companies. Those who founded or tried to form companies were defined as sinners and criminals acting against the government and the consumer nation. Any candidate whom Georgio liked received invisible assistance to his communication and production machine. What made Peugeot elected for a third term in a row.

"You have a meeting with the palace representative," the volunteer secretary called Peugeot. Peugeot had been preparing for this formative moment all his life and did not need the reminder of his secretary whose name he did not know and it was replaced like any secretary who finished her "service consumption" in the mall's elected office, It was very common a consumer was chosen to enjoy as a serviceman, and it was also a touristic experience for him. the career, work and the trip that was over after a week.

"I wonder what Gogol has to say to me, after all, no one else has been sent out of the palace, I'm sure he can give a

44

recommendation to the captains above to allow me to move to a position in the palace," Peugeot thought as his feet stomped to the floor without paying attention that Georgeo's representative will arrive in the next hour.

Gogol entered through the gates of the House of Representatives guarded by the "Private Police Company" which guarded all the mall state institutions. The policemen stood still as Gogol went head to head, agitated by his intense separation from his wife that morning. He went straight to the point with Peugeot, knowing there was no need for artificial formality from an experienced and knowledgeable politician like the one he was about to meet. Gogol mused on his way to the meeting: "An official conversation is usually made with a consumer - visitors who were not even aware of the people who pulls the strings," Peugeot was a puppet pulled in strings trying to drive its strings in the direction it wanted.

"We have a non-virtual device that we want to market in the mall. It's a device that will help you control and get elected and it will help us sell as much as possible."

"What kind of a device? Why do the hologram consumers have a physical device sold to them that could be destroyed and put a burden on the sacred balance of materials?"

Gogol quickly interrupted him: "Let me finish, we don't want to reveal to you all the capabilities of the device, but it certainly allows for an exciting emotional experience for the user in it. You've probably heard our preliminary publication, all we want is for you to issue a license for the device and take a picture of you using it with pleasure. "

 Peugeot snapped up again: "I don't know how I can issue a license for a device that runs on the human body? Surely it is that kind of a device, isn't it? A device that sits on your head? It seems dangerous to me, I should consider it, there will probably be a resistance." Gogol noticed that Peugeot's bargaining skills come to fruition, he didn't think Peugeot really cared about the health and well-being of the mall customers.

"It's really important that you cooperate, you don't want to stay in this mall all your life, you know if you get elected for the fourth time you will go back being a regular consumer." Gogol bluntly hinted to him, with his tired eyes, that were suddenly waking up and staring straight into Peugeot's opening mouth that seems upset.

Peugeot responded with surrender: "I understand the message. I'll set up a committee to test the device and I'm sure it will come to the right conclusion." Gogol tapped Peugeot's shoulder, left the device on the Prime Minister's desk, and quickly left the room, while Peugeot looked at the device that looked like a helmet fit for an average person's head.

Chapter 7

That evening, the White Palace was very crowded, everyone rushed back to their homes to watch the mall's holographic breaking news. No one expected the main headline of the news article to be: "A girl started an illegal business in the mall owned by Georgio." During the story that aired in Fox and Sunan's voice, Mazda entered through the palace gates, one hundred forty-seven dollars in her virtual wallet. The virtual wallet was activated with a chip that was already inserted into her body as she entered the mall state border, Mazda wondered if anyone could read her thoughts out of the chip.

As she walked down the corridors of the "White Palace of the mall workers" as she appeared on the palace screen, Mazda came across one of the staff members who ran to watch the holographic show, which is much more impressive by using the chip injected into the bloodstream and affecting the brain. The screening began, after which Mazda felt exposed as a perpetrator of a crime, which was in fact defined as a sin by the mall news broadcaster. She watched the screening as she was at the center of the "Central Hologram Clothing Store" where the broadcast of the news show took place.

48

As she watched reporters murmur about the girl who dared to
sin for money when her images were screened in front of her,
a shopkeeper approached her: "What is the gray thing you are
wearing? I imagine you should wear something a little more
colorful, such as my outfit." Mazda looked at the
saleswoman, and she was shown a hologram of a dress from
which purple, blue and pink stripes were puffed up in a shape
that was three times the size of her real body. A collision with
a hologram can only have one result: penetration into it, but
you cannot see what is beyond the hologram; the hologram
has been projected from stickers onto the skin that read
messages from the chip flowing into the seller's blood. Mazda
stepped back toward the store's door, afraid to recognize her
from the broadcast, and explained to her: "I came from a
place where fashion is irrelevant and clothes has no meaning
beyond covering the pubic body, that's how all people are
equal to where I came from or at least feel that way." Mazda
noticed that behind the 3D hologram projection a bunch of
people sat on benches and watched a projection hidden from
Mazda's eyes.

"Very pleasant, my name is secreta, come after me," the
woman told her. "In my opinion, you will fit into our store as
a saleswoman, but first let me dress you more appropriately
than you have been accustomed to this day." Mazda tried to
imagine as she was accompanied by the dressing room
salesperson how bright and colorful she looked to Sony. It

was hard for her to accurately imagine what this look would be like, where it would be no problem to create this particular attire, one only had to apply her vague dream to something invisible: "It's just one of our new designs that our designer has created in the clothing generator. Dazzling, but these sparks will attract all the shoppers in the store outside the palace. " Said Secreta looking at her delicate face and thinking how beautiful she was and how much attention she would attract. In contrast, Mazda imagined how such a move would advance her to a high-ranking priestess who jumped toward the highest floor of the White Palace. A goal every career person working in the palace would like to achieve.

Mazda was unable to get the name of the seller, but she found herself lagging around after her all over the palace as she received explanations about its departments. The palace was made up of four huge, white skyscrapers with hundreds of tiny windows flickering with lights. Secreta explained to her that red light marks a room in action, blue light indicates inactivity, and white light blended with the palace color so that the window cannot be seen because the palace was known to have bright white light. The upper end of the palace was gleaming in white, the shop manager pulled her hand with her right arm, marking her in the left arm that reaching the upper floors was her sole purpose.

50

Mazda asked her as they sat in the garden which the four towers surround: "But what is upstairs?"- The seller replied: "We, the shop managers are on the lowest floors, we run the companies that employ the lowest-ranking employees on the corporate floor. In the middle of the tower is the Holdings floor, this is the floor where high-ranking people spend their lives finding the needs of the residents and making as much profit as possible, for example, what holograms will be consumed, etc... "Mazda asked:" But what is on the top floor? Who gets the money from the holding floor? "

Secreta replied: "The top floor is called the stock floor, the one who is there sacrificing himself for Georgio until the day of his death. These people have bloodied for him on horrible missions and come out alive, they have the right to own a stock that belongs to George And get to keep it because it is very holy, only a hundred chosen people carry stock on their chest, they are the highest priests. Each of them has a special ability and talent with which Georgio is aided several times in his life. It's hard for me to believe, but maybe one day I would be well worth holding a stock, despite the slim prospect. " Mazda asked behind the manager's back as she pulled her into the tour towards the top floor: "Do you mean Sony the presenter, too? Does he also own a stock? Is he on the top floor?"

The manager ignored her question with a sour look as if she had a mental block to deal with such question, something in her brain prevented her from answering, so she answered with an unrelated answer: "You will never come here as long as you do not run a company, unfortunately, I am not allowed to enter the second floor because i Need a higher degree of holiness. Unfortunately, I did not earn enough money to be able to sacrifice the cash at the alter. Have you ever sacrificed your salary, You know you should not use your salary? Only this way you will gain an appreciation and the doors of the Job-Track will open for you. ," Secreta escorted Mazda to the reception office, where the decision-maker is expected to decide whether Mazda will work in the palace.

Chapter 8

Cisco came into Subara's room, knowing that was craving to see him not only as an assistant, whenever she examined him, dressed in his shiny gray uniform. He still hadn't imagined that the change in her body would make her take those steps. Indeed, Subara approached him and touched his chest with a smile: "Will you accompany me to the workers' dining room?", The queen exited the room as she pulled Cisco's hand out of her room. They marched hand-in-hand as they followed her along with the metal structures of the packaging company, which was a multi-room complex, and at the bottom, the workers put in the effort as the job required them, and their skills were adapted to it by a genetic supplement they received through food: some enjoyed repetitive physical work, some enjoyed data analysis In the face of the flickering display, and some enjoy being on guard as if loaded with certain watchdog genes that cause them to guard properly. Everyone received extra treatment from the genes that transcribe instructions to the blood inside their body. For the first time in a long time, there was one who returned to her human body configuration, it was Subara, the only one who lost the vitality of added genes. Already in her birth, her virtue was revealed as a perfect genetic influence for obedience and management that will make her the most perfect queen ever born. As she sat in the dining room, the

53

influence of the genes began to fade and her blood began to harbor more human emotions such as lust, jealousy, and domination. She thought, "Why food is not served in my room? And it would be better to have" non-gene-therapy "food that will bring me back to my humanity. It is time to treat me with the respect I deserve as a queen, isn't it strange that I eat here in the dining room like everyone else? She called him by name:" Swatch, take me out of the dining room and serve me the food in my study, please, "the word: "please" was said out of embarrassment because she scolded him, she felt that she was filled with new powers but was also scary, inside she knew that her natural feelings originated from the times of her ancestors. She whispered in Swatch's ear while collecting the food: "Don't collect the food from here, I want food that is not genetically modified to be given to me straight from the factory, I'm waiting for you here. As he descended to the factory he was preoccupied with her aggressive appeal. Subara rose from the dining table, she was one of the few historically-minded individuals and knew why gene supplements are put into the food of workers. She knew that her natural human capabilities would give her an edge over the rest of the bureaucrats and supervisors of society and that she would certainly leverage her constitutional dominance. With her unique capabilities, she can bend some rules. She imagined how she would be indulging herself in the pleasures of life worthy for a woman in her position and streamlining processes in the company so that she could take over the rest of the mall owned by Georgio.

An hour later, as she dined alone with Cisco who was looking at her, she noticed his sturdy body and handsome face and smiled. She was no longer worried about the company laws imposed on her as Cisco's manager and brainstormed how she would make love to him. She shared her thoughts with Cisco: "We need to discreetly distribute our engineered food at the mall to stimulate consumer sympathy to us because they normally have to eat tasteless pills that are daily subsidized by the mall's government. Not only will we gain their trust but make them loyal to us ".

Cisco interrupted: "You mean all of us, except you." And wink in a flattery manner.

Subara looked at him with an angry facial expression but immediately smiled: "Be careful or I will feed you with this fresh food, you know that you should not argue with the queen of the company, even if I am no longer under the influence of genetic food, do not reveal what I eat from now on!" She put down her eating utensils and kissed the stunned Cisco, he wrapped his arms around her as he was fascinated by her passion and beauty and they both lay on top of Subara's desk which served as a dining table. On that evening, the mall's dome color changed to orange. Subara was wrapped in a thick sheet on which she slept with Cisco and stood on the porch, looking down on her workers admiring the processing machines from the doorway in the dome: "I need more workers, we need a plan to save the mall's consumers

from their confiding and mesmerizing state, no more brainwashing but work and partnership fraternities."Cisco did not understand what she was talking about exactly because that partnership had been ingrained in him since he remembers himself.

"Don't you think the expansion will lead to imbalance and overcrowding in society? Why do we need a change that will cause friction with Georgio?"

Subara smiled at him and stroked his bareback: "You know, I always knew you were a man I would love to be with, you have a very smart outlook and a good overview. I will persuade you to stop eating from the food served in the dining room. In any case, I believe if we investigate and prove what happened in the fire We will have a great cause to come in demanding compensation from Georgio. "

"Why do we need Georgio's compensation? Who said he would agree?"Cisco felt embarrassed that Subara was

56

consulting him, he was not used to dealing with considerations pertaining to masses of people.

Subara said: "If it is a murder and not a fire accident, a war must be fought back."

It was an air-conditioned morning as always at the packaging company, the smiley and satisfied production workers of the company passed pieces of wood through the cutting machine destined for the mall's companies. Suddenly an announcement flashed on the screens, calling everyone: "Important message, please, gather in the packaging warehouse." Workers' families left their spacious rooms and swarmed to the company's gray corridors and metal railings. Mazda and her family left their apartment abruptly by the order of the announcer to move toward the warehouse where lights flashed. Their room was furnished only with the items they needed and never felt any need for additional products such as the sparkling clothes sold at the mall. Their modesty was due to the influence of the engineered genes given to them at meals served daily by the packaging company free of charge.

 While they are greeting the rest of the workers, it was just a case of a flu disease that had prevented Mazda from eating regularly for a few days, she fell behind her mother and brother and stayed behind the crowd looking at the screen as the special message "spokesman" of the packaging company appeared. While waiting for the announcement, the families of the packaging company workers were greeting each other and talking to each other. Suddenly the secretary's face appeared on the screen, the secretary raising his voice as the audience almost completely silenced: "It is important for us to warn you, my friends, for many years we trade with the mall without concern. We feed ourselves with engineered food that maintains our unity, in recent hours Our intelligence department has alerted us about external influence attempts from the mall. Broadcasts such as "commercials" whether they are sound or cinematic will try to infiltrate and take control of your screens and headphones. We are about to show you a soundless broadcast. " Then Sony's character appeared in the background, hugging a long and blue-haired girl, smelling her neck. Wearing silvery clothes and a leather-like belt fastened to his shapely loins, his shoulders broad red, he looks like a prince taken from a medieval legend. The girl wearing only a silk dress pulled out a bottle of perfume. Mazda was amazed as the rest of the audience in the special video blushed and felt a huge heartbeat as she looked at Sonny's face inaudibly muttering things that seemed like words of love. At that moment, a fire broke out in one of the warehouse walls, flames striking the startled workers looking for shelter. Few fled to the exit door from the warehouse between them was Mazda who was standing behind the crowd. The flame hit the door a few steps from Mazda, she stepped out and managed to slam it. One flame met with the other, which together formed a circle of fire around the warehouse where the crowd was trapped, inside was Mazda's family.

Chapter 9

Secreta waited for Mazda outside the decision maker's room, Mazda entered the room that was a hundred times larger than any sleeping capsule she ever saw in the big mall, on one side appeared two fancy red sofas, on the other a canopy bed put there for a very important person. The decision-maker asked Mazda to sit in front of his desk in the center of the room. The walls of the room were projected with flashing and colorful holograms that contained legendary and historical figures strolling around Mazda.

"Mazda, for what purpose did you come here?"Ask her diligently the decision-maker,

"To Work at the mall and to try to settle down here."

The decision-maker examined Mazda and while looking for information about her he said: "According to the data on your chip you arrive from the packaging company, you did not receive this chip at your birth but only when you entered the mall."

Mazda nodded her head: "That's right. I came here from the packaging company. I ran away because I felt something was waiting for me here."The decision-maker looked at Mazda

60

and said to her: "To really belong here, you only have to want one thing, and it's hard for me to believe that anybody from the packaging company will know what it is."

Mazda blurted out, "I came here to donate my share to the Alliance and..."

The decision-maker silenced her back as he banged his hands on the table: "No! The right answer is that you have come here to succeed, spiritual success. This is the goal of the mall's White Palace employees. You will advance here and earn as much as you can until you reach the highest position, that is how you will succeed."

Mazda looked down and said, "This is what we were taught at the packaging company, sorry, I will learn because I intended to stay here."

The decision-maker nodded: "It is nice that you managed to enter the palace for the money you earned, it is a nice sacrifice none of the consumers in the mall did. What I can do is give you a job to your satisfaction. I am impressed that you will fit to sell holograms in the mall store. I must be honest with you, if you are a packaging company spy, we will have no choice but to get you out of the White Palace, I won't take any risks. Now get out! "The decision-maker commanded her as he swung his finger toward the front door.

Secreta who was waiting for her outside the office smiled at her and said: "You are now starting a new path, you have been elevated to a sacred priestess saint for the integrity of the mall and I will therefore dress you accordingly."A flattering blue trouser that complimented her shapely cut was worn to Mazda's body with by a thought from Secreta's brain chip, she imagined the dress hologram Mazda would wear. Holograms are usually worn by consumers only. That was not the case for Company executives or production line managers in the White Palace, for them, raw materials were allocated to create physical and real clothing. Mazda is subject to a hologram dress code because of her role, the lowest level in the White Palace is the management of the hologram clothing store, it was the same role Materana has, as she manages the Georgio branch to purchase food pills. Mazda had one last meal at one of the White Palace restaurants where she was served meat-engineered food made from raw materials created by synthesis machines, the same raw materials that came from the packaging company from which she came to the mall. Two guards led her outside the palace gates as she noticed the blue garment appear on her body while walking a short distance from the store which was to run without any formal training. Mazda felt that she was returning to the starting point of her journey as if she had begun a hopeless period of imprisonment whose end is unknown. she will probably have to adhere to the consumer-career religion's rules in which she gives consumers service in order for her to reach the higher ranks in the White Palace. The wheels of creativity began to move in her mind, she thought of ways to help more consumers buy their clothes rather than in another store, in any case, all the stores owned by the same god-like, called Georgio. A few months later, Mazda's routine can be summed up in a lifetime of endless consumer service that only sucked her creative ability by focusing on convincing consumers to wear a hologram jacket or in their language: clothing. Consumers would come to the store to spend the rest of their money given to them by the government for "consumer worship" as defined by Georgio and his marketers, but the official term was a "minimum universal wage" concept invented about a century ago. This fee according to the mall state's doctrine was to be credited with salvation and considered a commandment, a ritual that was completely foreign to her but slowly she got used to. The same ritual was based on the idea that purchasing virtual products would bring them liberation and redemption and that the possession and accumulation of money or possessions in their possession would lead to mental decay and desolation. For example, she met one girl who screamed at Mazda not to close the store in the dead of night just when she was about to go to bed, she told her she should not end this day with another credit point that would be listed in the digital wallet in her body. Mazda felt sorry for that woman, even though she did not understand the intensity of that woman's anxiety. Despite this, she was empathic enough for her suffering to allow her to enter and reset her point quota, for which she purchased a reddish and slightly transparent hologram dress that suited her greatly. The woman let go of her anxiety until she forgot to even look in the mirror to see how perfectly the dress was placed on her body. Mazda felt lonely in her one-person sleeping capsule, a period of mass production, with herself serving as the assembly line. On those nights filled with insomnia in front of a capsule advertisement, she realized that she not only lost her family at the time of the fire but also the prospect of meeting her beloved Sony in the White Palace.

64

Chapter 10

At the ivory tower where Georgio was situated, the mall's dome was scratched by the edge of the tower. On the transparent canopy of the mall, a map of the world was drawn, so Georgio described the great mall as the whole world, embracing everything. On that day, the White Palace glowed with white light that brought back sunlight to the mall's dome. It was a long day of activity on the high floors of shareholders, the board convened for the monthly meeting on the highest crystal floor, in the White Palace of the World's Mall. Beneath it was the white floors of the shareholders who came in the elevators to the Crystal floor.

Georgio isolated himself with his baby in his room, a baby taken from the maternity room without first ascertaining the mother's identity. Georgio didn't really care, he also grew up in a company of a father that educated him from childhood to the point he was managing the empire. Every moment he looked into the baby's eyes, he saw his father's severe face that forced him to be hardheaded and control with a tight fist. The baby helped him keep some self-control and mental resilience, he emerged from his baby's room with his head held high, leaving him for the nanny's care.

The board meeting began when Georgio entered in an impressive hologram suit, all at once, the shareholders stood up with a glittering stone worth of a share hanging on every one of their necks. After Georgio, Gogol and Intelan came in and sat down on both sides of Georgio's long table. The mall's police secured the entrance to doors that were closed anyway to anyone whose chip does not match the stand. Intelan began by saying: "Your Honor, It is written in the journal that we need to discuss the marketing a physical and unique product for the mall, in terms of development we have reached a final level of" emotion vacuum cleaner ", given the packaging company's resources we are supposed to allow ongoing marketing of the product at an even price, the only question is... "

Gogol stopped him: "Sorry, Intelan," he said with a stuttered voice, "we should call it an" emotional reader " and Not by any means under the name" the emotion vacuum cleaner ".

Georgio interrupted Gogol's remarks, saying, "You are absolutely right Gogol, but let Intelan continue its economic-technological explanation."Intelan waited for silence for a few seconds and then went on to say: "The manufacture of the device, as it is physical, will open the mall's dependency of the raw materials on the packaging company. In addition, a technical support system should be established. Limited in budget and because I watch... "

66

Georgio interrupted Intelan's remarks: "Don't expect anything. What is planned here is a change of order in our favor and strengthening the worship of believers, when can you start producing the device regularly?"

Intelan answered him immediately: "We have set up a production line in the last month and we can start at any given moment."Gogol waited for Intelan to finish and then went on: "Dear and Honorable Sir, I will ensure that all shareholders are updated to the priesthood and below as far as the new product marketing system is concerned, and most importantly, I have obtained the approval required by the government to market this product."

 Georgio interrupted Gogol and asked with a glance into his eyes: "Did you lower the tax from the administration on the new product?" Gogol replied: "Sure! The new device will have zero taxation. The Prime Minister promised us this in accordance with the terms I set him, sir." Gogol faded a little, he was always insecure when he made promises to Georgio, as he did to any authority, but to Georgio, he knew that his present life depended on an accurate and responsible answer. The session went on for a long time and dealt with many details, it ended as usual with all stock priests voting without exception for the plan. The session was over, the revolutionary plan was underway, Georgio knew that the lives of priests and palace managers were about to change, not just his own life. He marched with Gogol and Intelan and also joined Pixario, who is responsible for all of the artistic prowess of Intelan's technological products. He ensured constant output from the best palace artists who produced the finest clothing and costume holograms, and also conducted the preparation of the best entertainment and new productions presented to the mall's consumers on screen while they are awake and the massive bombardment of silent commercials while they are sleeping in their bedroom. Georgio asked Pixario and Intelan to access their subsidiary floor, to continue the vigorous work of designing the "helmet" product, namely "the reader of emotions." Intelan, who was anxious and fearful by nature, did not know how they were going to set up a device that needed raw materials for it and was several thousand times bigger from the chip inserted into the body. Also, Pixario, the artistic director did not know how to design a helmet that would catch the eye and function properly because the heads masses Have a different head structure. On that day, he didn't think he would have any other concern for himself, especially for himself, but also for Intelan and the army of engineers at his disposal. Gogol felt lonely walking beside Georgio, although he was almost 8 inches tall, that day he felt particularly humiliated and bent.

Georgio asked him, "Why do you look powerless to me?"

Gogol replied, "If I can share with my manager, I will thank you for that. You know I don't have anyone to share those feelings, my wife left our apartment and left me a message that our relationship is over,"

Georgio tried to show empathy, but instead, his words were filled with empty words of encouragement: "You have to keep calm, you're the only one I have to rely on to do this job, now that we're facing far-reaching changes in the entire mall! You'll soon be the only one I want to contact him. " Saying these obscure things, Georgio disappeared in the elevator to his right, leaving Gogol wondering what he meant. When Gogol returned to his apartment, he re-watched the hologram presentation that Adoba took with her camera, he heard the message: "I live in a housing unit in the White Palace at the design department, I don't get the attention I was used to getting from you and so I leave, I feel hurt and lonely and Yes, I'd rather feel it away from you, where I will have enough busywork and distraction without the transient encounters with you that only cause me pain and frustration. " About a second after Gogol watched his beloved's message he felt something he hadn't felt in a long time, at that moment he realized he was sacrificing himself too much, but the sense of fear he felt because of Georgeo overcame every self-will. Gogol decided to go to the design department to check on the progress of the helmet design but really there was an internal urge to approach his wife employed there.

Chapter 11

In his mind, one of the consumers saw the store from the inside, where Mazda was selling holograms to customers. he watched a news article using the chip in his body about the wonderful helmet that is attracting shoppers to the stores, a helmet that would allow reading the emotions of others. The same consumer who was Swinging bachelor immediately put a smile on his lips and imagined how, in his slick words, he would enchant the best women who would fall into a delightful relationship with him. He walked into Mazda's shop and was very impressed with her beauty and smile, the flattering gaze that the tall man radiated from above was not new to the Mazda who was accustomed to customers of the opposite sex who were amazed by her. She ceased to smile and hoped he would immediately apply for a new garment, so she showed him the five new collection clothes. The consumer asked her to turn off the holographic screening and told her to listen to him. She looked at him suspiciously and he said: "The rumor is that you make custom-made clothes, do you?"

Mazda hesitated and immediately replied to him: "Of course, you will have to pay above the usual fee and send me your request from your chip."

70

The slick customer answered: "Do you want to hear a news item that will benefit the both of us? I will not waste our time telling you, they call it a" reader of emotions ", it will give you the opportunity to sell to my kind and myself included. The first device will be marketed from the White Palace courtyard and allow to deepen emotions, one to another, without suspicion. " She stared at him in disbelief, because of her love of designing clothes, she began to design a 19th-century blue regent's suit tailored to his high height and shoulder width. He looked at himself in the mirror as the golden epaulets thickened his shoulders and on the suit flap were prominent and impressive gold buttons. At first, he felt strange and peculiar, but a few seconds later he had the confidence to step out of the shop, feeling that he was the general of the mall on his way to another conquest.

He returned to Mazda and asked her: "Where did you get this amazing design?"

And she replied to him, "From the history books I learned from in school,"

 The consumer asked her: "What do you mean you learned from books? Did you not have access to all the information you want on the chip? And what is the school?" Because she was a graduate of the packaging company elementary school, she did not want to disclose her origin to a regular consumer and therefore politely said goodbye to him. The useless knowledge that had accumulated in Mazda's memories and was inaccessible on the big mall's intranet* network was an exclusive source of information for her, memories that came to mind in her sleep. She was inspired by the medieval knight's armor, the dusty leather suits of the cavalry led by Ginges Khan, who even crossed the prairie with her. She restored an ancient Strait clothed with Cleopatra gold jewelry. Consumer audiences were amazed to discover the ancient world before the world's holocaust. Every client who consumed a garment stood out in its uniqueness without knowing that his ancestors wore the same garment because without the historical context the same Mazda models seemed to be taken from fashion designs according to Georgio's theory of consumption and marketing. As far as consumers are concerned, every item purchased has no meaning to its content and what is important is its very consumption that brings them to do a holy good deed, this is the wheel of life in the mall. After several sales cycles at Mazda's store, the mall's department store manager looked at Mazda's sales data and marveled at the yield. This was a huge increase than ever before. She thought she should hire her as an assistant in the White Palace and sent Mazda an interview invitation to the chip in her mind. As Mazda dressed a group of boys in black monk uniforms, she was summoned in her mind. Those young men who were stunned by the uniqueness of the uniform were left disappointed in their physical gray clothes when she turned off the holograms and asked them to leave the store. They were expecting to be inspired by the aimless rebellious spirit of those black hooded black uniforms they could cover themselves from the mall's surveillance cameras. The leader of the group who saw Mazda move towards the walls of the White Palace turned his gaze toward the group and urged them to move on. She didn't know what to expect at the meeting with the principal, whether she would be ousted from her position or whether the meeting was an opportunity for her to get promoted higher in the White Palace on the way to her beloved Sony.

Before entering the gates of the White Palace, she looked away, watching the band of boys wearing black monk's clothing on her advice. For the first time, she saw the charismatic guy lead the pack as he donned the headdress that distinguished him from the group that surrounded him. Mazda immediately realized that these were computer hackers who miraculously managed to steal her design, she had no other logical explanation for why they were dressed like that without buying anything from her.

* Intranet - the internal network, as opposed to the international network.

Chapter 12

Virtual and digital attire is the biggest asset and a source for self-identity to the loyal consumer who believes in Georgio's rule. It is no wonder that the fashion design department at the White Palace was the largest of all development departments. Gogol walked over to this ward to locate Adoba, he knew she hadn't lived in their apartment for several days and was afraid she is spending her nights in a capsule outside the White Palace. As he walked down the corridors of the development center that is at the base of the White Palace pyramid, he saw around him departments delivering virtual products to mall customers that they would purchase in exchange for satisfaction points. The same points will be used by giving a command to the chip that flows in their blood and interfaced to the palace's intranet. Whether it is the acquisition of stories such as "Georgio's rise to greatness" written by Georgio, or whether it is the preacher's demand for participation in virtual purchases using the universal salary that each citizen receives each month for his account. What is important is that the balance between taxes and income will always increase for the benefit of the great shareholders of Georgio. Gogol walked quickly into the White Palace fashion department, where talented fashion designers were covered in black glasses to prevent external disturbances and created from their feverish minds thousands of "tailor-made" clothing styles in virtual reality made of bits and bytes of computer code, the same software developed decades ago and still used by the big mall for creating naked-eye sealed hologram outfits. One of those female creators who was fortunate to emigrate to the White Palace due to her talent was Adoba, who met Gogol a decade ago as a designer assistant who sent Georgio's uniform to the chip in Gogol's mind. He fell in love with her delicate, breezy smile and elegant cut and white virtual silk wrapped in her profile picture. Ten years later, he finds himself physically approaching his wife Adoba, trying to find out why she left him but in vain. The touch of his hand on her narrow palm surprised her, she immediately turned off the projection of the blazer she was working on, the blazer for the charming and young consumer, intended for consumption by the mall's bachelor men, although they were not intended for her use, she could imagine the average man displaying them. She disengaged from her dark glasses and looked straight at him as she focused her bright eyes at his brown eyes: "I'm not coming back to you, I went to sleep here in the virtual office of my employees, my manager called me here, our relationship ended when you disappeared from my heart."

"It's really eliciting my empathy, I have to admit." Gogol replied, "But you have to understand the stressful situation I'm in. I need my wife when I get home, a warm hug at bedtime, and someone who will disperse loneliness. It's hard

for me to imagine anyone but you who can do it, Adoba."
Adoba had known her husband's poetic and diplomatic wording for years and was not impressed. Just wanting to get away from him as much as possible, she ran forward toward the hall so she wouldn't have to deal with his selfish whims. He found a message sent from her to his chip: "Even when you come back to do some courtship you do it so brutally like an elephant in a china shop."

Adoba continued: "Understand, on the whole, I want to express the creativity in me and my longing for you when you are on missions. I came to realize that you will not change, you are an adrenaline addict at work or it is your fear of your boss that makes you put me in second place. Fortunately, my longing gives me the power to create "Art is the study of my inner feelings and also the study of culture that surrounds me on the outside." Gogol, stunned by her harsh words, took two steps back as he looked sideways at the design artists who were concentrating heavily on the screen projected on the dark glasses they wore on their eyes. He looked inside into Adoba's soul and realized he had no place in her life. Adoba returned to her work with tears streaming down her cheeks, where it felt like it was a sedative for her aching heart. Her workplace to which she could flee the fastest without suffering, she hoped it would have sheltered her forever without her knowing the future to come for the designer's wing.

Chapter 13

The raw materials cargo hovercraft flew through the exit of the south wing of the mall where the packaging company was located. According to the lease agreement for the property in which she was sitting, the packaging company was obliged to supply raw materials and food to the White Palace. The White Palace guards who were a cross between the "Great mall's Democratic Alliance" and the "Southern Carton and Raw Materials Society" did not even suspect that the hovercrafts who flew above them were overloaded with food, and had to be subjugated across the mall's corridors. Subara did not plan to change the structure of the subjects of the white palace, this would only further establish their loyalty to Georgio. Alternatively, her simple plan was to expose the inhabitants of the palace to solid foods that would shake up the senses of the consumers of pills and intangible holograms. So it was that a family of five: a couple of parents, two daughters, and an elderly son, walked along the long shopping avenue. Suddenly, a box of cardboard that was slightly crushed by the thumping of the ground fell over them. The youngest son went first to the parachuted object, touched it, and examined it. He glanced anxiously through the slotted, slightly crooked cardboard wigs if the family scolded him to stay away, but it was too late and the boy's hands were smeared with a sweet-sour sauce of mashed potatoes. The boy did not hold back when the strong smell made him drool, he immediately pushed his fingers into his mouth, the chain reaction triggered a few hormonal reactions with a smile on his lips, even before his parents could get close to it he was already opening a larger hole in the cardboard and tearing his wigs more and more in front of His amazed middle sister (the older sister looked in the window of one of the new dress brands). The boy pulled and removed chicken thighs from the crate, he had no idea if it was once a living creature or a genetically engineered product made in a factory, but the sauce covering it and the bread crumbs made him sit on a nearby bench and tear its skin and flesh. The father was the second to go to the carton and before him, he discovered a variety of bread, pasta bowls in tomato sauce, a pile of vegetables and fruits, on the other side and in the center was the mashed potatoes and a good amount of sausages covered with sauce. Even the father and mother, who were at least fourth-generation pills-only consumers, were amazed at the magnitude of the impact that this pile had on their bodies. After a few hours of gluttonous feeding, the counter-reaction of their cramped stomach began to affect the family, and they threw up on the mall floor what they had accumulated in their stomachs. It was a great and varied physical pleasure, much like the lovemaking he and his wife had the other night. In fact, their new sense of satiety was more powerful than the feed pills ever did and they looked at each other with a naughty look that even their older daughter felt embarrassed about, already sixteen, and knowing such looks from other boys in the mall. If not for the smell of vomiting in their mouth, the parents would ask their children to wait in the corner and let them pair at a sleeping capsule. After all the family members washed their mouths in the nearby fountain, concerns ran through the father's mind: "Maybe this is a test of consumerism or maybe it's a test of stealing a non-tangible object?" After all, something so different in the mall has never landed that its whole purpose was to serve as a worship center for Georgio. In fact, their only pleasure is derived from the consumerism that has increased Georgio's wealth.

The father warned his family not to approach the cardboard box: "We may have failed the test that others have faced, and we will never reach the redemption of the White Palace, we have succumbed to our passions and taken something without purchasing it."

The son felt ashamed and said: "Sorry Dad, I hope Georgio won't be angry and punish us." And finally, like all the residents of the mall, this family also succumbed to the sinkhole of consumerism that gripped them from their birth because they were only human beings.
While they were moving toward the shops they saw one displaying a doll in its window with a gray helmet covering

her head to the forehead and back of the neck while the doll's ears were exposed.

Chapter 14

Manpowerena watched Mazda entering the room in awe. At first glance, she was unable to see through her, even though she had the skills and experience as the company's human resources manager. To get a feel of her candidates, she would occasionally send an early opinion on the candidate before the interview and then talk to him while being recorded when his personality and abilities were revealed to her. In 99% of the cases, Manpowerena was right, this time too, she noticed a creative and sensitive girl who excelled in her role as a salesperson, not because of her trickery, but more because of her verbal ability and the right look. This came from the informal dress that Mazda wore, as well as data she gathered about her that were not part of her sales statistics. For example, she learned that Mazda sold many clothes, not from the official collection but those that were defined as "other", hence Manpowerena concluded that she designed them, nor did Manpowerena have data on unsatisfied customers, that is, she would not trick them. From this, she realized that a classic candidate for the "Emotional Reader Helmet" was in front of her. Manpowerena sent Mazda to the training room, where Mazda learned about helmet operation without a detailed technological explanation. This is a complex system that absorbs and transmits information from the chip that is in the bodies of all the residents of the mall. The helmet can process brain information and inspire energetic power on the helmet wearer so that he can decipher in his mind the feelings of the people close to him. The helmet has a short-term ability to absorb physical activity from other people's chips. It has not been disclosed to Mazda that the helmet can induce a hallucinogenic state similar to the intake of drugs that flow into the bloodstream, and also mentally draws the subconscious. While assembling the helmet, Mazda did not feel it, because she did not think of any special creative thought, the true purpose of the helmet was: creative information mining, Mazda felt pleasant and obscure like with a drug influence, she was not in the process of creative thought and therefore no data was absorbed in the main scientist computers. Mazda removed the helmet as she didn't understand what was happening to her, the helmet stopped working with her brain, she knew she was facing a fascinating new future, and excited about the prospect of being a pioneer in the field that would lead her into the White palace's ivory tower in the future. Manpowerena turned to Mazda: "I see that your brain works well with the helmet. What you have just experienced is just a preliminary test of the prototype. With your permission, I would like to test your creative skills in a group of experimenters. Please accompany me." The two women came out of Manpowerena's room with Mazda holding a helmet. She did not know where Manpowerena was taking her but realized that she was probably participating in the helmet experiment and that she had to prove herself properly, she did not know how to prepare for the event, Nevertheless, every limb in her body was prepared for what was about to happen. Manpowerena left her in the professional hands of the White Palace engineering and development team, Mazda was told. She and about ten participants were dressed in actual physical clothing made of synthetic material, a very strange feeling for people who never wore anything but a hologram made of laser light flashes. The staff wore the helmets to the participants and explicitly instructed them to drift in their imagination, close their eyes and try to read each other's feelings. On the other hand, the training manager whispers to Mazda's ear to control the team as much as possible, while they would, without their knowledge, drift into an associative thought that is actually Mazda's commands. Mazda didn't understand what the supervisor meant, but she closed her eyes obediently as she hoped for the best. From here, she found herself marching with her subordinates as everyone wore metal armor from ancient times, but what surprised her the most was that they found themselves standing in the middle of an open field. She was the only one who truly admired it because the rest of the group was in a state of dream and believed that this is the reality, as we all know, usually, if someone wakes up from a dream, he remembers its contents by how strange that dream was. Mazda never experienced the sun beating down her face nor the touch of the fields that tickled her feet, yet it seems that her imagination conceived this event and transmitted it into the helmets of the other participants in the experiment. This case where she is the only one aware of what she is fantasizing about and they are dreaming has given her the power to lead and influence the event. In the distance, an ancient Gothic castle on a mountain was visible, Mazda walking toward the tall building and the rest of the group accompanying her. Mazda knew the reason why they were walking towards the castle, to reach the seat of Queen Isabella. The country they walked in was in the province of Castile which is in the land of Iberia, Mazda brought this historical fact from a lesson she attended at school as a child. She believed that the impeachment of Queen Isabella from her rule would stop the flow of historical events that changed the world and led to the destruction of many peoples. This thought came to Mazda's mind as she contemplated the event that had come true as an act she had attended at that moment in most of her wonder. The Palace Guard commander ordered the group to stop, Mazda understood from what she was told in Spanish according to the commander's body language. Mazda insisted on letting the gang pass, she ordered everyone to continue and the rest of the group swooped on the guard. After a bloody sword fight, the many guard soldiers fell under the band's sword. Mazda did not mean that violence would happen for them to reach the castle but did not control the conduct of the group, most men and women had violent instincts which caused them while dreaming to attack the guards. Only five women, including Mazda herself, were left alive after avoiding an encounter with the force of the guard as they were leaving the sword in their sheaths. As they climbed the stairs to the top of the castle, a huge gate was discovered in front of them, Mazda instructed the four remaining soldiers to push the gate as the other side of the castle was discovered where Queen Isabella sat alone. The queen wore a red silk dress, with a diamond-studded crown, a pink scarf around her hair, and a cross on her chest, tied with a necklace to her neck. She lowered her head, waiting for Mazda to raise her voice towards her. As Mazda approached the queen, before she could open her mouth, a man burst into the room wrapped in scaly armor and a sword in his hand. When she looked at his face, she saw that it was Sony the celebrity endorser who was the object of her love shouting at her to stop. Mazda woke up in amazement at that daydream, ripped the helmet off her head, and took a deep breath as if she was rescued from a dive in a deep ocean. One of the technicians removed her helmet from her head and placed Mazda on a treatment bed. Mazda looked terrified at a huge screen that the technician team manager enthusiastically pointed out, the manager presented to his team the results of the experiment: Creating literary art written by the computer according to Mazda's dream photograph. The team had the script and the full-length movie of the entire dream. "Really a wonderful dream dairy!" Said the team manager excitedly as he passed the data over to his superiors.

Chapter 15

The election period is over, and the prime minister's election day is about to end. According to voting data streamed through the internal chip from the mall state's consumers of about 88 percent of the voters, the big winner of the election was undoubtedly Peugeot. To that end, Fox and Sunan were sent on the coverage and interview mission of the elected prime minister. Sunan's intention was to present a flattering coverage of the elected prime minister who, to her knowledge, was Georgio's favorite candidate. This is how the candidate whom Georgio delights to honor will be reviewed. Fox was biased because of Sanan's body and suspiciously adopted her views, and it did not occur to him that Peugeot's election was made following a conspiracy by the White Palace. He tended to believe that Georgio was a father figure who was watching behind the curtain and contributing to the mall economy that no one has control over. This is how he was taught at the White Palace Journalist School and had no chance to think otherwise.

The volunteer secretary called on Coca to go into the PM's office, Coca was Peugeot's former secretary, who knew how to attract him with her charisma and beauty as well as her conniving ideas. Coca reminded Peugeot of himself what made him emotionally attached to her, and their conversations were enjoyable to him. At first, when he just met her, he looked at her purely sexually as another substitute secretary whose name he did not remember, when she would bend over and lean her back to pick up something from the floor or when she looked at him in a naughty smile when he left to home after a long day at work. To win her presence after her volunteering term was over, he hired her to serve as the Minister of Finance in his government, she served as a loyal minister in his government, a helper fit for him. his legal wife and the general public did not know about this arrangement.

On the day journalists came to interview Georgio, Coca was sent to an important meeting in the White Palace with the bank's lobbyist of "The bank the united of companies", the same bank also provided accounting and financial management services to the "Democratic- companies Alliance's of the Big shopping mall". The lobbyist sat in her office as she waited for their weekly meeting and she looked at the company's financial data. The door opened to Coca, she smiled at her sparkly smile that attracted the attention of The lobbyist's heart and made her focus on her presence. As a successful woman, she also appreciated the success Of Coca who managed to get into a management role so important at the big mall's government.

The lobbyist-priest opened: "I have invited you to my office to discuss the taxation you will impose on our companies during the current administration."

Coca stroked the lobbyist's hand gently: "Leave this serious conversation aside, tell me what's been going on lately."Coca tried to evade the conversation about taxation even though she knew the lobbyist would soon dictate to her the exact percentage of taxation approved for the number of mall consumers. This is the budget approved by Georgio for the mall government. The lobbyist said in her voice the message that was transmitted to her through the chip in her body, a broadcast coming from the top floor of the palace. She tried to sound formal but friendly as she conveyed the message to Coca. She was fascinated by Coca to a great extent, Coca knew that there was no point in arguing with the lobbyist and that Peugeot depended on Georgio's mercy, even if it was at the cost of the government budget. "If there is a consumer nation, then the one who rules them is the manufacturer," Coca thought to herself as she left the priestly lobbyist's door. Coce's next stop was the White Palace's Private Academy, an initiative by Georgio under the guise of an education grant when, in fact, academic points were sold in the form of degrees. At the same time, besides the profit accumulation, the title content was invented to establish Georgio's rule. Professor Microscope murmured at the sight that broadcasts to hundreds of thousands of chips, a broadcast designed for students across the mall and the content of which was the bi-weekly course sermon. He tried to ignore Coca's presence. Coca, for her part, ignored the importance of the sermon the professor delivered and lightly touched his shoulder to get his attention. For the professor, this was one of the most important lessons the college could give to freshmen: "The Beginning of Consumer and Purchase Theory." The professor ignored her touch and continued to read from his memory: "In the nineteen-eighth year of the first century of consumerism, thousands of companies were scattered across the earth and the country was in chaos. Around them, people were wandering among the shops, flooded with scam advertisements."

After touching his shoulder once more, the professor turned around and went on: "Now we will learn about the new Georgio Mall commercials" and he broadcast the commercials while addressing Coca: "Why did you interrupt me in such an important hour when the crowd listens to me?" the Professor Scolded at Coca.

Coca answered him with a fake smile: "You know I have to keep you updated on the syllabus at the beginning of each term. I have no intention of desecrating the sanctity of the rule's book." She walked with the professor to the academy cafeteria. As they walked, Coca saw the paths of the other faculties intended only for palace workers: the bookkeeping

90

faculty, the computer science faculty, the art faculty, and the fashion design faculty. Somewhere in the hallway leading to the basement of the building, the Faculty of Literature and History, a remnant from the old universities before the global ecological disaster that smuggled the survivors into the big mall.

The interview with the elected prime minister began, Sunan and Fox sat down in front of him with a mirror over their heads photographing a hologram of everything going on.

Fox tried to raise a boring question: "Mr. PM, congratulations on your victory..."

Sunan burst into his words: "Is it true that you intend to extend the business license to companies to allow them to sell physical helmets in addition to holograms marketed so far?" Fox paused, waiting for PM Peugeot to answer Sunan's question. He bit his lips in frustration and thwarted his feet.

Peugeot replied: "The helmet project is unbelievably important. It is a real consumer product that puts consumers' minds in place and allows them to reach amazing emotional capabilities. I have no idea what exactly the helmet is supposed to do, but I believe it is a reader of emotions."

Sunan interrupted the PM's remarks, saying, "A very important product for politicians like you, isn't it?" And winked at the PM.

Fox broke into the argument: "Reformist circles say you are deliberately lowering the tax to the White Palace at the expense of consumer welfare at the mall." The question hit like a bomb in a bunker was said in a loud tone, and there was silence afterward.

The Prime Minister replied bluntly: "This is a speculation of political interests, the White Palace has always been to the service of consumer citizens. Taxation is calculated in such a way as to make it easier for consumers in the mall."

Sunan pinched Fox in the arm and interrupted PM's remarks: "What about a new fashion office? A promise to open a fashion office to oversee consumers looking to buy new pieces of clothing "Fox, attracted to Sunan's beauty and extroverted character, was heartbroken. He knew she was motivated to become a media critic for the White Palace media company. Such questions would raise her profile in the eyes of her bosses. Fox continued to remain silent throughout the interview until the end, moving uneasily in his chair.

Chapter 16

The line towards the helmet store lengthened and split into adjacent streets, there wasn't a consumer who did not desire to feel its beloved feelings, a proper replacement for natural bouquets that did not grow in the mall but fairy tales praised.

A couple walked into Mazda's shop and approached the counter, the woman asked: "Does the helmet really allow you to read emotions?" Mazda replied in the affirmative, she was forbidden to discover the truth and share her own experiences. The guy who accompanied the woman asked Mazda if the helmet was a hologram or just an object. Mazda gave the couple two helmets that were immediately put on their heads.

She guided them to close their eyes and empty every thought from their mind and then whispered to them while their eyes were closed: "Try not to think of anything but my instructions, then let the rest of your mind flow freely. Slowly, your emotion will fill and you will find that the helmet absorbs feelings around you, and turn them into thoughts you can recognize. "

The guy jumped enthusiastically with his eyes closed: "I feel your love for me Phillipa" and hugged his partner. The couple hugged and kissed passionately, while his helmet glowed red and her helmet glowed blue. Mazda felt jealous, she never experienced intimacy like the one before she felt. She, too, wanted a man to hug her warmly, remembering her late parents who only hugged her a few months ago before she disappeared inside the big mall. The guy stopped to cuddle and whispered to Phillipa: "I hear in my head how much you love me, it's a very strong emotion,"

The woman moved away from him and said with her head bowed, "I hear no emotion from you, only jealousy from the girl across the booth."

The girl rushed outside with a sour face followed by the surprised guy, the last words Mazda heard from them were of the girl: "Be sure we won't sleep in the same capsule tonight." Mazda, who was obliged to put on a flashing helmet on her head, allowed herself to daydream as long as the store was empty of shoppers. While fantasizing about her embrace with Sony, she couldn't help but feel a transmission of data and flickers from her helmet, feeling that she couldn't go out of her daydream and even opened her eyes and couldn't see clearly the reality around her. It was a double observation of daydreaming and reality, only the removal of the helmet from her head caused this visual doubling to cease. When it was time for the store to close, Mazda returned to the White Palace, where her neat work-room was waiting for her. This

room was prettier than the one she had in the packaging company when she lived with her parents and certainly fancier than the consumer advertising capsule. Her room was full of holograms broadcasting advertisements all around the room. She relished the ad channel that only broadcast Sony's products, so she fell asleep in her cozy four-poster bed. In the days that followed, a growing flow of consumers and white palace workers arrived at the helmet store. Mazda worked endlessly with hundreds of consumers, most remembered by her were a pair of doctors working in the palace and their children who visited the store and suspected the biological damage that might be caused by wearing the helmet. "What are the side effects caused by helmet use?" They questioned Mazda with questions full of medical terms she couldn't answer. Their loyalty to every brand that came out of Georgio's factory remained intact and they purchased "family helmets" for the family. However, Mazda reflected on her heart, did there exist a motive that was hidden behind the slogan written on the store sign and preached "reading feelings for public unity"?
At the end of the day, a group of boys in black monk's clothing who were known to Mazda from the clothing store she worked for walked into the store.

The head-covering guy who led the group turned to her directly while removing her headgear and said to her: "Hello, my name is Rayban, I and my friends are sure that you know us from somewhere." Rayban looked at her with a playful smile.

Mazda answered him: "I probably sold you something in the past."

Rayban replied: "I'm not surprised that a pretty girl like you serves as an ornament to Georgio's kingdom. My group is trying to break into the mall computers and get holograms out of them. We even managed to put our hands on a hologram projector, but I'm curious to know what is the physical product that you are selling here."

She remembered where she knew him from: "Why should you steal an intangible product like a hologram, whose value is nil and is distributed to all consumers a dime a dozen. The Holy Scriptures say that Georgio rescued us from the shortage."

Rayban interrupted: "I hope there are enough helmets for all the residents. My friends and I will be happy to purchase helmets from you." As Mazda turned to open the drawer in which the helmets were printed with a secret code she typed, Rayban's friends in black robes wore the helmets that were on display and left the shop without paying. Mazda was startled by the hustle and bustle of the store, but unfortunately, she could see the empty display, and the last of the thieves,

Rayban, fled out. Around the ruined shop backdrop, Mazda's desk stood in front of the door, a hologram projected on the table, showing the store's helmets stock and their location. Mazda did not call the mall police and no anger showed over her face. She just remained curious about the gang of rebellious boys. The group reminded her of herself, from the time she wanted to open a grocery store. She curiously followed the display of the stolen helmet movement across the mall.

Chapter 17

Subara woke up from Cisco's embrace, walked over to the mirror, and looked at how her human face was revealed to her like the times she was a child before she was fed the genetic-alternation virus. As she wore her presentable suit, she had a sweet, bitter memory of a girl destined for greatness and a dream about working in the field of robotics. Already then, the idea of being a robot operator was appealing to her whenever she was watching the packaging company engineers sent outside the Great mall Dome for raw material collection missions. Unfortunately, she was forced by the College Board to follow her mission as a future queen and attend the Faculty of Government and Political Science. Recalling the dreamy girl who suffered teasing from the kids in government classes, she turned her head to Cisco's voice lying beside her in bed: "Do you have to go to a college speech?"

 Subara approached him and shook his naked body under the blanket: "Don't forget that I have assigned you a lab recruitment task." Cisco had trouble waking up after Subara had already left their apartment.

Subara was accepted by the College Scientists with great respect, she stepped onto the podium as those present in the hall eagerly awaited her opening: "The Packaging Company's College was established by its founders to provide an equitable education to all. Their children were taught robotics and Political Science according to our worldview. I intend to continue the policy of sending each child to study in his or her faculty within studies that include accommodation outside the parents' quarters. The children will be fed with genetically engineered foods with a gene therapy virus that will shape their personality to serve the packaging company. " When she finished her speech, Subara went to the laboratory of the Head of Nano-biology Sciences.

Subara met privately with the professor, who was not used to visiting company leaders, for years he was responsible for perfecting the maintenance and preservation of those genetic components without any political oversight. His instructions stemmed from the packaging company's ideology of maintaining the equality of the company's worker's genetic capabilities. Company employees were supposed to each have special skills, he was prohibited from discriminating against any of the children to be left out without genetic fingerprint. "I need you to find me the most domesticated and faithful animal genes, a predator species, the most aggressive humanity has ever known." The professor did not know whether he should feel awe or panic at her demands before he could even think about the significance of her demands, rose from the habit of his natural taming, and moved toward the genetic library. The genetic library contained millions of stem cell samples, it was a physical collection of blood samples that had not yet been collected in the laboratory's computerized system. As Subara followed, the professor went to the Predators Wing and from there to the Dog kingdom subdivision. Used in this division to distill samples to generate gene-coding for docile behavior, these gene-healing tablets were placed for all packaging company employees. Subara was interested in more specific sampling, and indeed the professor handed her a transparent box on which the word "Pitbull" was written.

The evening fell on the cladding windows above the robot development labs of the packaging company. Cisco walked through the entrance to the lab. He toured among the engineers who were engaged in assembly, construction, and development work that only a collective buzzing sound came from their nostrils. The sound was a side-effect of bee-type genetic healing. Cisco glanced at the line of engineers, suddenly saw one of them knocking nervously in the background and furiously throwing away the tools and chips she was working on.

"I'm not ready to continue under these conditions! An engineer like myself may not have to work with such old-fashioned equipment!", Cisco stopped the security guards who threatened to take the engineer out of the room with the foreman.

He whispered to her to stay quiet: "Everything will be fine, I'll take you away." The engineer fell silent and bowed her head as Cisco led her toward the foreman.

"This is not the first time she's raging like this." The foreman approached Cisco with a serious face.

"She has uncontrollable anger, last time she kicked one of the employees."

Cisco replied to the manager: "In the Queen's Palace she will be treated with the other offenders. The Queen is interested in order and efficiency in the packaging company, which is exactly what I came for,"

The foreman nodded his head in affirmative and replied to Cisco: "I would love to have more violators if you will find any. This time he shouted out loud that all the other workers would hear. Cisco and the engineer left the academy building.

On the ruins of the burned lecture hall, the best offenders of the packaging company gathered. They were sure they were going to be severely punished for their actions, they did not imagine that they would be trained for the most difficult job they could ever imagine. Once concentrated in a desolate area, they were instructed by Cisco to disperse tents on the ground. The area was paved with marble figures, embossed with the mall state emblem. Around them were the remains of burnt concrete piles and lead, a reminder of the severe attack that occurred there by the terrorists of the Big mall Company. Cisco made a speech while standing amid the wreckage, where hundreds of packaging company employees were burned to death. The future soldiers underwent arduous fitness training while the ushers whipped them with flashing electric rods. From day to day a new breed of warriors developed, the frustration of the bondage leading to uncontrollable anger, and in combination with the training they became fatal war machines that in the day will be given weapons. While resting in tents, they were fed into the secret ingredient, which contained the genetic code that would make them bloodthirsty human-Pitbulls.

Chapter 18

At the top of the white palace's ivory tower, the upper white room flickered in a yellowish light. This is a sign of information system overactivity. those systems present data in a holographic matter to the corporate leaders. Georgia looked intently at the acquisition data concerning the helmets, he seemed dissatisfied.

Gogol, who was watching the data with him, began apologetically: "I understand that you are appalled by the lack of the emotion reader helmet's purchase, and there is also a decrease in the purchase of food pills."

Georgio puffed his mustache and was about to leave the room: "Wait a minute sir," Gogol shouted to stop Georgio: "There is a slight increase in the purchase of holographic clothing and educational content, and the customers who believe in you may feel guilty for their lack of response to purchase helmets and food and therefore buying more clothing details. "

Georgio interrupted him: "It is a top priority to sell helmets. You must find a marketing method. Read the marketing holy book from start to finish until you find a solution!" Georgio ended his roar.

Gogol blocked Georgio's path: "Sir, you know I am well versed in oral marketing theory, I do not need to learn it again. An excellent solution would be to give what was previously called a customer loan, meaning money that does not exist on our balance sheet in exchange for interest, the loan will be given only for the purchase of helmets! ". Georgio pushed Gogol and disappeared through the door, entered his hover, and flew to the mall's view. Whenever he was anxious and worried, Georgio entered his hover, sailing alone as he pondered quietly. Gogol did not realize that Georgio's family secret was kept with him, only Georgio knew the true historical story of the great mall that was passed from one heir to another. The big secret was that the collapse of the global loan and credit system had caused the previous collapse of his family-owned company. The collapse of the banking system and the ecological collapse of the outside world a century ago caused the Big mall to become a haven for survivors. Georgio's great-grandfather decided to run a closed economy with a limited budget of 1 billion Eullars without growth, which left the mall stable and protected and with a cardinal rule: no credit system can be maintained at the mall. Georgio looked at the video of his old baby son straight into his little room and immediately ordered his shuttle to be diverted. That day he spent with his son as he sat watching him, absorbed in his thoughts. During the reflection period, Georgio recalled his father sternly explaining to him about the mall's financial system, being grounded for ten days just because he had not done his homework for his private teacher on time. Georgio took the leash off his son, after his father, Georgio the first, who was so tough in his education, decided that a change in the economic system could bring him a little more power and control. Georgio's sense of omnipotence increased as much as he could imagine, now that his father had passed away. Georgio left his son's room and went up to the control room where Gogol and the other counselors sat. Intelan has proposed a plan to transport nanobots to create an innovative assembly line of physical products that will be stored in the White palace's Central Bank vault. Gogol, on the other hand, stopped him and offered a method of credit that would be run by the wisdom of the masses An experiment that's already been done on the palace workers. Data and public knowledge of the best educated in the palace and historical scholars were brought by the main computer of the big mall company, Gogol smiled and looked sideways proudly at his initiative, while Intelan looked down at his disregard for his plan. Georgio and the other advisers read with admiration when they saw the graph that represents the amount of intellectual knowledge that was extracted from the helmets, it was a cumulative knowledge of years spent in the minds of the palace workers. Gogol believed that when he was allowed to start the free-of-charge pilot of the helmets on the professors, it would be the groundwork to perfect the knowledge of the palace. He was pleased to see his spiritual father Georgio satisfied with the economic plan, in fact, the computer presented sprinkled collection of thoughts of professors who did not know that their memory and education were so easily exploited. Georgio silenced the commotion created by the brainstorming in the air, all silenced by a speech that none of the participants knew when it would actually end, all in the light of Georgio's angry look who stare toward them: "We must unite interests, we cannot let an outside company compete or threaten us, certainly not new competitors to threaten our existence, for this we need an iron grip on the most important infrastructure of the Great mall: the human resource. After the unused human material becomes a useful raw material by mining information, we can control the media and we will not allow To subversive forces mocking my big name. "

Gogol listened, he nodded, until he burst out: "Your big name is ahead of you Georgio, all the mall's consumers see you as a king, if not a god. We will never go back to the ancient days when they mocked the ruler."

Georgio raised his hand and Gogol was silent after he said: "So-called satire must be directed to a public official and not to an undisputed ruler like you if your total ownership of the mall would not have been a choice, so any media messaging in your image is irrelevant and even considered a blasphemy". Georgio ended his speech by saying: "We must use the credit program as an emergency only, from which we must return to the previous stable state." Georgio turned his gaze to Gogol in the last sentence, he felt Georgio was not completely satisfied with the credit plan. He swallowed his spit openly as Georgio turned away from him and left the room while the other participants remained frozen in place.

Chapter 19

The corridors of the mall were laden with flashing signs that flew through the air and changed their shape every second, to read the sign on every beat one should have concentrated completely. One in a thousand was an advertisement for a loan sprawled on the signs that were produced by colorful flying nanobots that threatened to become the eternal working-class according to Georgio's vision. Mazda roamed the corridors completely ignoring the flickering signs. She tracked the flashing spot on her locator, which was given to her in the White Palace for tracking helmet stock every time a wave of shoppers crashed on her doorway. Mazda used this locator to navigate her way to the helmet thieves, they were the few who dared to challenge the convention that prevailed at the mall: "Georgio is the nation's savior, a living god, whose the mall's free subjects are entitled to elect their representatives and leaders. The subjects have the freedom to purchase everything that Georgio sells to them, the one that protects them from the companies that once ruled the mall and caused the world to be destroyed." This philosophy was memorized in Mazda's mind, the packaging company's refugee. She was delighted to have the opportunity to work in the palace and get herself promoted until she would have reached an aristocratic rank of tenure alongside Georgio. It was just an excuse to hide Mazda's real desires, the biggest of which is her encounter with Sony. It was hard for her to forget about the social education she acquired from an early age at the packaging company school, and yet she truly believed in the texts naturally used by the mall's consumers. While pondering, she ran into a nanobot loan sign on her way, but it paved the way when he recognized that she was a white palace worker and was selling helmets herself. Other mall consumers came across a flashing sign and took a $ 99 loan to buy a helmet. The ones who got to buy and wear a helmet seemed to sit dumb while their eyes were completely bleached, their veins protruding in red as they sank into their imaginations within the fantasy their mind produces, cut off from the world around them. The helmet connected their dreams to their consciousness while with a wide smile enjoying watching the imaginary film that they are the directors and screenwriters. The helmet directly pumped the neuronal information from the nerve end of your head as binary information to the White Palace intranet. No one of the mall's consumers knew his imagination was being processed, analyzed, and turned into a virtual product for resale at the big mall. Mazda noticed the significant change that had happened to the consumers of the big mall. The mall has ceased to be a bustling place for consumers who are eager to buy and wait for their tomorrow Eullar stock to be renewed. The mall was filled with helmet wearers sprawled on the walls and cut off from what was going on, which increased the alarming silence of the huge space. Mazda noticed that the stolen helmets appeared every time elsewhere on the locator's monitor, from here she realized that the thieves were sending confusing transmissions of the helmet location through their intrusion into the intranet. Mazda decided to use the thieves' signal transmission by connecting a helmet to the dream it transmits to the main computer. She sat down with a family that included a couple of parents and two small children, all four of whom were big-eyed and with a wide smile on their faces. Like them, she closed her eyes and continued to daydream from the stage where she imagined her meeting with the Queen. From that moment she plunged deep into a sleep forced on her by the helmet worn on her head. In her dream, she felt herself standing again in a spacious hall where Queen Isabella, the queen she had studied in history classes at school. The queen ordered her guards to take her to the darkest dungeon in the darkest basement, Mazda did not understand the meaning of the punishment but she did not fight with the guards. From that moment, she thought she had to connect bi-directionally to the helmet of the thieves. The guards left her arms, she felt a blow to her forehead and fainted, when she woke up inside the dream where she saw the five thieves sitting in a dungeon. Everyone was crouched with no movement except for Rayban who approached her, so she figured he was the only one operating this dream and the rest of the characters around him were just a figure of his imagination. Mazda woke up and Rayban's location flashed in the form of waypoints on the small monitor on the helmet. Mazda immediately removed the helmet and ran toward where she knew where Rayban and his gang were hiding. Mazda immediately recognized the points on the map, it was a store that was closed and not yet operated by the big mall, she discovered that it was a store in branch number 128. Upon arriving at the hiding place of the group, she fearlessly burst into the room beyond the virtual door which became opaque in color, so Mazda passed through the hatch and saw the group sitting laughing among themselves. The boys examined the helmet they stole and anyone who noticed Mazda began to giggle at her, pointing to her angry face. Mazda immediately recognized Rayban who smiled at her calmly, she did not realize that he was looking at her as a beautiful woman who attracted him.

"What kind of consumers are you? Did you not know that a limited edition of such helmets must not be stolen. From the place I came from it is not allowed to steal at all, everyone contributes with his activity and work and shares everything he has."

Rayban chuckled with the rest of the group: "It's absurd that you call us consumers when we have no part in the consuming circle. For us and all other unemployed subjects. Yes, that's what we are, unemployed and non-consumers. That's the old nickname for our situation."

Mazda did not understand the meaning of unemployment, she regarded it as disrespect and defilement: "I strongly condemn your words, we are all a part of the sacred class of consumers. Why do you insist on focusing on the inaction rather than the consumer action on which you receive minimal universal pay from the government?" She almost mumble a threat to expose them, but memories flooded her mind. She imagined her childhood with her family, pictures ran quickly in her mind, tears flooded her eyes, Rayban's words seemed to affect her, and she remembered old words against the big mall she learn during her schooling at the packaging company. She turned and walked quietly back towards the palace, leaving Rayban and his group completely uncertain about their fate. Another uninvited delivery from the packaging company plummeted across the mall, those of the residents of the mall who owned helmets were too mesmerized to enjoy the plunge dropped for them as a so-called gift.

Chapter 20

Cisco's armed thugs, aka "The Packaging Company's Liberating Army" have crossed the unmarked border of the beginning of the Great Mall. At the southern end of the world, the sun's rays glowed through the glass ceiling. The sun dazzled the group's eyes, they covered their faces with hats and dark glasses. With this scary look, they intended to clash with the consumers of the big mall. The thugs who split up all over the mall stores were under the command of Colonel Lockheed, who ordered to keep the safety of the entire mall's consumers and to attack only armed police. A few hours later, walking through the mall's stores, looking at the herds of consumers as dozens of them fell into a deep sleep, with a strange dream helmet on their heads, the colonel realized that there was no reason for a police officer to come and protect any of the consumers. The police are not meant to protect the civilians, they are meant to keep the order, and there is no order like the state of being asleep. While shattering the glass of windows with their electrified batons, it turned out that the smashing effect was none other than a hologram. The contents of the stores were empty and projected with clothing holograms. The most offensive thing the thugs could do was disable a piece of projection of the garment from some of the mall's consumers who had not yet slept. The gunmen were unaware that this was a daydream and not asleep situation, it was a reinforced action of the imagination with maximum concentration that prevented the helmet wearer from any contact and communication with the world around him. Colonel Lockheed was helpless with the unexpected situation, the dog-like vigilance that flowed in his blood dissipated and was replaced by the memories of his early youth rebellion when he was a hasty student who used to walk alone without his parents' supervision. His father used to work in mines and forests outside the mall's dome, he was sent by the packaging company to dangerous mining missions that took months off the packaging company's walls, before it was run by robots. Lockheed's mother, a sick and weak woman, lay in her bed most of the day. Like every family in the packaging company, he lived with his parents and three older brothers in a spacious apartment in a gray, high-rise building. The doctors who frequently examined his mother claimed that radioactive radiation-toxic substances had brought her to her morbid condition, probably due to his father's travels to the polluted outside world. This hypothesis that his father harms his mother caused Lockheed the child to be angry with him, which in his adult life developed into a fit of anger towards the world and his closer surroundings. He used to run outside the state school walls, usually during school hours, socializing with gangs of children like him. The pain he felt as a result of his mother's condition, which she had to endure for the benefit of the public, led him to a sense of frustration that he used to riot with his gang. At one time equipment was smashed and scattered along with factory food while workers were on a break, and once computers and electronic tools broke down in empty classrooms. When he graduated from high school, his mother died, and the rest of the graduates turned each for his appropriate job of serving the company, Lockheed continued to socialize with his group, this time to gain strength and profit. The group feared many of the top officials of the packaging company, all-knowing that a tax, food and appliances, and special services should be given to the head of the crime organization. Lockheed wanted to escape from his father and family's old stomping grounds, trying to find new adventures in the Big mall, that it was said to be: "The free market enslaves the human spirit for its materialistic nature." Lockheed marveled at the many fancy stores available to mall consumers. "Their job is to serve the mall only as consumers in the living budget given to them by their government." Lockheed thought to himself: "So far, I've been robbing the packaging company's collective warehouses, maybe I'll rob stores?" Indeed, this is what Lockheed's soldiers did as humans with dog instincts, beating people to make their way through frightening consumer queues standing in front of stores. They shot the crowd in the street with a psychotic amusement coming from their human side still in their image. The mall police officers used a limited-power electric shocker that could cause at most a temporary warm-up to capture undisciplined consumers, but did not have the power to fight Lockheed's soldiers, so they hid or fled to the White Palace. Lockheed ruled that he must stop this devastating turmoil, for the first time in his life he resigned and did not rebel. He grew older in his mind and now that he is far from his family he has built himself a new world through which he can manifest himself as a true leader. "Move soldiers!" Lockheed shouted, "We are moving towards the government building, take a seat on the train." The soldiers made sure that no consumer or palace worker was left alone on the train, the train quickly reached the Prime Minister's building, Lockheed marched his soldiers into the building, from where he would send a new order that would not be dictated from above, hoping that they could continue to produce engineered food to satisfy his hungry soldiers. Peugeot, the mall's prime minister, heard the reports of the approaching force and made sure to head straight for the White Palace. Peugeot lost control of the government budget, as he became an expatriate and inactive prime minister. "What about consumers who depend on their consumer budget, and what about the state of the mall?" Thought Peugeot accompanied by Coca, his loyal secretary as they escaped to the gates of the White Palace. Lockheed sat comfortably on the prime minister's armchair, with the clerks' command offices in his reach. He managed to communicate with the officials and ministers even without political power, the government budget was in his hands, all but the means of production. "What in the power of the White Palace to do now? will Georgio be a powerless religious priest?" While

Lockheed messed around with his thoughts till it was raising steam across the room, the company's leaders have been summoned to an emergency meeting at the palace. Georgio's meeting opened when the conference room door slammed straight after the terrified Coca and Peugeot entrance.

Chapter 21

The meeting was particularly heated, the best of experts sent the best ideas across the room. Gogol sat beside Georgio listening as he glanced over his left shoulder and saw Georgio lose his patience, cold beads of sweat dripping down his forehead. An idea shone in Georgio's mind, he silenced the audience with a loud scream as he moved sharply from a sitting position to a standing position with his head raised. The crowd fell silent, it was a long-standing vision that unfolded from his grandfather's days and before him from the days of the giant companies that ruled the world before uniting into a huge and closed mall.

Georgio began: "This is how it will be from now on because a belligerent mob has forcibly seized the elected administrative position, and so we, as the sacred and sole economic society with my celestial management, have been forced to bypass the monetary system that was until today." The crowd mumbled incomprehensibly as Georgio stopped talking. Georgio raised his right hand up and the crowd went silent.

He continued: "The idea is to distribute an alternative form of payment to the official currency of the state to be honored by us for the purchase of any product our company markets.

118

Because we control the market, the official currency of the state will lose its value and use." Intelan sat down, listened, and could not resist, standing up to say despite his fear of the leader: "Sir, it is not technologically possible to bypass an existing currency, the only currency to make transactions with is the state currency, we would have to distribute our wares for free..."

Georgio looked furiously at Intelan who took a step back and answered him with a surprising smile: "Intelan, I'm glad that you as my Chief Technologist are aware of the technical functioning of the system. We intend to distribute free products in exchange for using points that will be honored by us, the amount to be billed for all transactions for tax purposes will now be zero Eulars " The audience opened his mouth in astonishment at the revolutionary idea that was originally Gogol's idea. Intelan was horrified at the technological challenge it would pose for him. Once again, he experienced great torment after his ideas were rejected while Gogol's ideas were accepted. Even now he must make a plan he does not feel comfortable with its implementation.

As a child, Intelan was forced to plan an online store project for the school, the purpose of which was to think about the content of the store to attract numerous buyers. He had to try and think of marketing ideas to increase the amount of shopping. Already at a young age, his exceptional mathematical mind was thinking in engineering terms. When the project he submitted was treated with disdain from the teacher, he was scolded by the whole class and was hurt to the core by the scorn, the waving hands, and gaze as he wanted to explain the way his shop worked. The teacher scolded him: "Your store is a shame and blasphemy for all pastoral priests. Nothing will come out of you." Eight-year-old Intelan's store was devoid of products and in fact, was only computer software that recorded product names and presented them as priced, it was built as a virtual store that will be broadcast to the eyes of all mall residents. Because he did not conceive any product, he received a zero score without any reference to the effort he put into building the store. From that day until he was admitted to the Academy of the White Palace, Intelan tried hard to become a great marketing manager and salesman, but all his attempts were unsuccessful. He had to go on to the Academy of Engineering, to the great disappointment of his parents. Twelve years later, he received a degree in Mathematics and Computer Science and began his work as chief maintainer of the White Palace's information systems and chip management. The sense of worthlessness and spiritual failure has lingered in him to this day, where he was given the task of creating the new credit program for the mall.

At the end of the meeting, Intelan went to his office in the main technology wing, sat down, and began thinking about a prototype for the new system. A female worker came into his office, he was in a dejected mood after the oppressive sitting he went through and was flooded with memories. Her beautiful face slightly raised his mood as he looked up and listened to her: "The mall's credit system is depleted of cash, the new military regime seems to have withdrawn all the money from the system." What Intelan's employees did not know was that the new regime at the mall was also working to change the virtual credit system and in fact found a replacement for the Eular system in the form of cardboard bills printed in the packaging company. It was the invaders' attempt to bypass the mall's virtual system. Thus, two monetary practices were created, which undermined Georgio's plan against the invaders to his large mall. With the cardboard notes produced from the packaging companies' boxes, every consumer can buy tangible products, except that the big mall has no such products except helmets and nutritional pills. The dog-men soldiers with the aggressive instinct made sure to take control of the parachuted packages dropped from across the big mall, scattering them through payment of cardboard bills to create a market for tangible food and clothing. In addition, the packaging company mercenaries brought with them tools such as quarrying shears, tree-cutting shears, etc that overwhelmed the imagination of mall consumers who had never seen them before, in contrast to the white palace workers who were supplied with many consumer goods. The packaging company soldiers forcibly seized control of the big mall stores as well, pushing away civilians who came to purchase some helmets with virtual coins or other currency.

A bloodthirsty bunch from Lockheed's soldiers gathered around the desk in Mazda's shop. Her first instinct was to run away, but on the other hand, she was interested in talking and identifying with them as coming from the same packaging company.

"Do you feed on engineered food? If so, where do you get it from?" Mazda tried to start a conversation with the group of soldiers who ignored her while they had searched for some goods in the store.

One of them nevertheless referred to her: "Well done, have you eaten transgenic food?" He spoke to her and winked with his doggy face: "You look like a white palace princess."

 Mazda answered as her hands on the service desk shook: "I am originally from the packaging company, I have infiltrated here a lot before you did and came to serve here at the mall." Mazda realized that the pent-up aggression in these soldiers could erupt at any moment and decided to take action and flee the store. She ran straight toward the door, and fortunately, the soldiers continued to ignore her and collect helmets from the store. As she ran, her head turned and saw one of the soldiers lying on the store's wall, engrossed in hallucinations as a helmet worn on his head.

Chapter 22

The riot in the White Palace continued, crowds of workers felt the sword of layoffs against their necks. The horrors of the violent takeover of the mall dreaded them, and also the fear of being immediately expelled from the palace. One lady, a graphic designer, mother of three, who was not one of the talented designers who feared the dismissal of the majority of the palace designers intensified from the day she began using the dream helmet, saw through the helmet a perfect three-dimensional graphic of a dress that no advertising designer could create. It was the computing power meets the imagination or if you want the user's subconscious. The same designer stumbled upon the terrified Mazda at the entrance to the cafe. With her sensitivity and intuition, Mazda felt that this woman, like her, was in a shaky state of mind.

A split second after colliding with each other's shoulder, they began the conversation: "I'm afraid they won't need me as a helmet seller or other products seller," Mazda pitched a note in the air that aroused interest from her friend

: "I am appalled by the developments in my life, there is no telling how my children will survive financially outside the White Palace. I fear for the fate of my children if I become a consumer, especially under the rule of these soldiers." The woman shed a tear and whined in her voice. Mazda ordered two cups of coffee, the woman's feeling of murmur increased as she noticed how beautiful Mazda's cut was compared to hers, and how much she wished to wear a flattering dress hologram offered by the clothing chip. Mazda listened intently as she stared into her reddish eyes, tear after tear, without asking her name as her lips moved and recounted her existential anxieties. She supposed that the same woman probably knew Sonny as the star of the commercials, and she may have been the graphic designer herself of those commercials.

"My name is Giavanshi," she reached for Mazda's hand, ready to shake, with a tiny smile straying over her tears-soaked face.

Mazda opened her mouth in amazement and her big gray eyes opened up to look like round and shiny wheels: "My name is Mazda, nice to know you, I have to ask you if you have ever been the graphic artist of the perfume advertisements in the White Palace? Do you know Sony?" Mazda couldn't help but be blunt and direct, sitting in front of a woman who could fulfill her dream. After the small talk of wine sips ended, Giavanshi reached for her hand and pulled her while they mutually giggled reaching into the main tower elevator. She took her into the depths of her study, where she intended to present to her pictures of samples she designed. "At the Big mall, the work is sacred, a privilege and not a productive goal. The entrance to a career hall felt like entering a prayer hall. The aroma of holiness in the air is interpreted by the nose of whoever sniffs, Mazda opened her eyes and saw thousands of huge screens in the graphic artists' room, there were dozens of edited and unedited pictures, with a snap of a picture of her Sony, his smile looking from the background as he was in a running position with his body tilted forward, his light hair fluttering and the dimples on his face bright as his slanted eyes are wide open, Giavanshi squeezed Mazda's gentle hand to sit in front of the computer development systems as she goes to her manager. A beautiful, thin, dark skin, woman with red hair spoke to Giavanshi and then went to Mazda: "What do you think about our excellent work? Do you realize that we have a very meticulous edit here? "

Mazda enthusiastically interrupted: "I never thought that behind the commercials that Sony appears in, there is a lot of computer work, it seems that Sony doesn't really look the way it appears on the screen."

The manager pulled Mazda out of the chair and sat down. She couldn't stop typing on the touch screens, with the buttons on them. While she was manipulating holograms,

126

eyes cramped as she communicated through the chip in her blood with people who were not present in the room.

Giavanshi explained to Mazda: "Do you see the stains and changes in Sony's body on the screen? They are probably the result of a hacking whose origins we are trying to find out."

Mazda said, "Is this the first time such a thing has happened?" Mazda was amazed when she saw the flaws in the commercials and came to her mind that the hacking was made by the same gang of boys who stole the helmets from her shop. Giavanshi was too preoccupied to listen to Mazda who decided to solve the mystery herself and left the White Palace to do so.
Rayban knew he and his band would soon be paid with a visit. In his mind, he continued to break through and sabotage the big mall's advertising mainframe, his group facing holograms of portions of characters from the commercials and distorting them to an unrecognizable state. As Rayban broke into the White Palace computers, his creative friend Nico thought of design solutions to distort Sony's image. Of course, no one in the group dared to distort Georgio's image. They were housed in an abandoned store that had long since ceased to serve the needs of the mall, surrounded by the packaging company fighter battalions. Rayban utilized the store's communications interface to hack the mall's supercomputers, its initial stated purpose was to free him and

his friends from the chipset in their bodies, but over time the target was replaced by the large white palace and mall symbols. Mazda passed unscathed among the packaging company soldiers, most of whom are sprawled with their backs resting on the wall and a helmet on their head, draining their imagination and consciousness. Mazda burst into the store and surprised the group.

Rayban with a smile on his face came up to her: "I knew you would come back, I have a suggestion for you."

Mazda yelled at him: "Not only do you steal helmets and break into shops, but do you also dare to grimace Sony's face?!"

Rayban put his finger on Mazda's mouth and remained silent: "If you want to move forward we will help you to report us, provided you do not really betray us. We will help you impress your superiors and allow us to continue our activities." Mazda objected: "Your idea is ridiculous. I will not let you hurt the advertisements of the Big mall for any reason."

Rayban replied: "You don't really care about the mall, you just want to meet Sony someday."

Mazda furiously abandoned the shop and answered them: "You're wrong, I'm not betraying, you will soon be caught." And she walked back towards the White Palace.

Chapter 23

Gogol went into the penthouse and found it empty, he didn't even call his wife Adoba, something in his heart told him she was gone. He sat down in front of the large window and replaced the view of the mall landscape with hologram presentations related to his daily work, to distract himself. His inability to enjoy the scenery was due to the terrible feeling of loneliness that went down on him. He went over the helmet distribution figures in the palace and noticed a 90% increase that astonished him and a small smile came to his lips. It turned out that the helmets were flying off the stand by most of the large mall's consumers, but the remaining 5% who used the helmets were non-official soldiers who were in control of the mall. Another statistic of the virtual currency was of great concern to Gogol, as he saw that the use and distribution of the new currency fell below 15%. Gogol reflected on a bitter face and finally concluded that this indicated a return to the Eullar, but the Eullar was not to be used regularly in the economic system due to this hostile takeover. If so, there is likely to be an exchange-traded on the ground. Gogol opened a communication channel for Georgio so he could immediately report the findings to him. The second he saw Georgio's scowl, he realized that he had to embellish the situation and show him the bright side of the helmets purchases. Georgio didn't even show a smile, he felt in Gogol's frightened voice that he was hiding something, he ended the call and waited for the final report. On the other side of the line, Gogol ordered a small flying ferry to take him outside the White Palace, straight to the corridors. He was full of curiosity but also worried, he knew that he had to leave the ferry with a supreme sense of victory, but today he felt a loss, his only victory was over the feeling of loneliness. "It is rare to feel victorious when you are alone, without anyone Who supports and applauds you." he thought.

 As he walked down the mall corridors he thought, "If my success is entirely for Georgio's goals, and he does not value my success then what is the value to everything I did? Why did I lose my loved one?" Gogol felt so gloom that it hit him in the gut. As he looked up, he saw a soldier handing pills to one of the mall's consumers and in return brought him what looked like cardboard bills. With his initial instinct, he realized that this is where the problem lies in distributing their digital currency, he quickly called Georgio when suddenly stopped the signal of his wife's location. He realized that she had stepped outside the palace into the Big mall and that she was motionless, a few steps from where he was standing. Gogol began to run through the shops, pushing families, soldiers, couples walking through the corridors innocently. When his chip signaled for him to stop, he stopped in front of a sleeping capsule store wall and noticed that Adoba's name was written on the monitor. Immediately a message was sent to him from Georgio that its content was: "You see she is not there, I released her from the palace in exchange for a helmet..." Gogol opened the capsule and saw that it was indeed empty, he touched his forehead, closed his eyes, and searched with the help of his chip for adoba's helmet location. As soon as he got the coordinates, he ran to the location on the map where the helmet is on his wife's head. He ran, took the train for a few minutes with all the crowds, and finally found among the plethora of helmets users lying on the wall of one of the shops the one who looks like her body. The helmet hid her face and her hair was folded inward into the flashing helmet, which indicated an intense brain activity. The helmet glittered in Adoba's head materialized into real sights, but she was aware that the world she saw was imaginary. At the same time, she completely ignored the physical world around her, even her husband's presence. In the virtual world, she saw herself sitting in an office, many years before the establishment of the big mall, when people lived in the open air and worked in office buildings only about a third of their days. Adoba found herself working on an outdated computer system, holding a keyboard and mouse, even though she had never used these tools, with a keen intuition to operate them. On the computer screen, she used her graphic skills in different ways and different designs and enjoyed every moment. It was the fulfillment of her shattered dreams after she was fired from the White Palace. In this world, the workers wore tailored cotton clothes and their lives were crammed with work, consumerism, family, and back again. At school, she learned about the life of the ancients, and now with the helmet, she could escape to such a world, an escape that was so much needed in those moments. Gogol, who looked at her paralyzed body that was rested on a wall, was filled with anger. Nestled in it the slight doubt that it might not be his beloved wife as long as a helmet covered her head.

At that moment he received a message from Georgio, the content of the message was: "I have integrated Adobe into the graphics wing fired list, as you know there is no need for an extensive graphics wing but only the editors of the works brought from the helmet users' content repository." The message had a painful continuation: "You know I care about you, so I took care of you and your functioning. Removing your ex-wife from the White Palace will only improve your work and keep you away from painful and unwanted feelings." Gogol was filled with frustration and decided to take action. At that time, Adoba continued her imagined life in an air-conditioned office in a computer graphic design firm. She was dressed in a tailored feminine suit made from the best chemicals that covered the face of women who wanted it at the time. At the end of her workday, as she went to wash her face, her head lifted to reflect her wet face. Her reflection in the mirror changed to a screening of Gogol, her husband turned to her with the message: "Go home, unplug the helmet." Gogol, who penetrated the chip into his helmet database, managed to sneak into Adoba's hallucination, if only for a few seconds. The message worked, Adoba cut off her helmet and removed it from her head, she seemed to be in a severe state of trauma. Her face was pale and around her eyes appeared purple circles that looked like the headlights of a boxer who had lost a battle. Gogol who caught her helmet noticed Adoba's strong attempt to pull herself back. Finally, without words, she held her helmet tight and ran away quickly from Gogol. Apparently, she had nothing left to say to her ex-husband.

Chapter 24

Subara and Cisco lay in their spacious bedroom, surrounded by crowds of flying hologram screens displaying every corner of the packaging company. Subara read Cisco's feelings with the help of the "Emotional Reader" which was an early version of the helmet received from Gogol, the White Palace representative. She absorbed a sense of deep fear wrapped in a more external layer of security, comfort, and warmth that he felt as a result of cuddling with her. The prototype of the helmet worn by Subara conveyed his expressions accurately and without distortion. She knew that his unconscious fear was because he was hiding from her the secret of the military failure of the takeover attempt he had organized in the Big mall. Cisco, for its part, feared being punished by Subara, who at any moment of her warmth could turn into a brutal cold blow and a painful rejection. Rejecting the moment when he told her about the army's disappearance, which was awkwardly addicted to helmet use, the military's physical strength was trampled under Georgio's mesmerizing computing power. Cisco wanted to overcome his fear, he tried to connect with the feeling of the man supporting his little wife who needed protection. Cisco felt threatened by Subara's political power, which was 10 times as much as his sense of masculinity. His mental castration made him want to prove himself to Subara, but would such proof eventually cause a break in their relationship?

 Subara got up from her bed, waking Cisco from his daydreams: "I had an idea that would bring our society back to prosperity," she said excitedly. Cisco was diverted from his reflections and listened intently to his partner, "I thought the packaging company would not only provide the material needs of the big mall such as raw materials, etc. but would be a fertile ground for cultural creations that would attract manpower that we would transform into our diverse humanoid forms." Cisco was happy with Subaru's idea of diverting her anger from the military failure to engage with another. Cisco consciously felt that he was a hybrid of a man with a dog who had to obey all his partner's orders. Despite the frustration of their relationship inequality, obedience to every subara's command eased his anxiety, because he had been tamed at the "Order of Obedient Children" twenty years earlier. In a school where they fed him with engineered food that incorporates into their genome with dog-taming genes. Cisco, who was one of the most outstanding students, continued to voluntarily consume the engineered food dedicated to him in the government dining room after graduating and continuing to work for the company. Cisco never missed his parents who abandoned him when they worked as physical laborers in one of the company's factories and were fed the genes of an Oxen. Cisco found closeness and comfort in his employers who were delighted to receive loyal and intelligent employees. He moved up the corporate ladder with enviable speed until he reached the head of the company. Subara instructed Cisco to focus on a new mission while reading his fear with the "reader of emotions". She figured out he was very worried about a particular discovery, she realized that it was the military failure at the Big mall, but she chose not to respond angrily to Cisco. After becoming a complete human being, her role was to take care of the collective survival of her subjects, despite her long-lost sense of natural maternal kingship. For this reason, Subara focused on a new cultural content creation task for the packaging company. She pointed to one flying screen showing what was happening in the packaging company's closed wing. The closed wing had treated opponents of the regime, agitated in their souls or those who could not digest the engineered food to serve a useful role. Cisco visited the wing alone, he saw people suffering from anxiety attacks and those that the packaging company refused to treat. He met a woman who had stopped functioning and suffered depression over the loss of her daughter in a fire. She was crying nonstop and was relentlessly imprisoned in one of the closed wing rooms. Cisco felt little mercy in his heart when he saw the woman, as he recalled the orders imposed on him by Subara, he debated whether the release of that poor woman from the cell would benefit her or whether the mission he will give her it would burden her. Cisco met with opponents of the regime imprisoned in the wing, after a short conversation with them he realized that they were opposed to the "the genetically impacted people fraternity" imposed on the packaging company citizens. Some would believe in a consumerist religion and on their cell wall hung a picture of Georgio, their only idol. "They appear to be physically strong workers, but the stronger your opponent is, the harder he will be targeted," he thought.

Cisco led some of his soldiers along the corridors of the dark and closed wing, gathering people for their teasing or distress and despite their emotional well-being. The former prisoners were taken out to the desert beneath the sun and forced to eat transgenic food, standing in line, until having an Agama Lizard biological properties. For those who refused to eat, the food was injected into their vein. Without blinking an eye, Cisco, whose face is covered in a helmet with sunglasses, ordered his soldiers to send the agamas to search for significant historical items scattered outside the Dome of the mall. Cisco knew that the soldiers would die in the heat of the desert and that only the Agama lizard men would be left just as the remains of the still trees in the scorching sun to be collected by the packaging company workers. Subara did not understand why the former Agama people did not return to the big mall after the effects of their transgenic food expired. She sent a bunch of nanobots flying over the desert, locating the agama people. Thus, about ten of the Agama people who turned back to a complete human form found an oasis and lived in it. Subaru watched the screen in her room as they met their mission objective: a remnant of a 20th-century car, a 19th-century weaving machine, a 17th-century military statue, a medieval knight's armor, and more, they were all painted with a special marker to be collected by the nanobots. "Now I have to put together a museum display that will attract different audiences, maybe I'll wait to find more sculptures and much larger buildings." The nanobots landed over the rolling chassis

of the car, dismantling it and carrying it as an energetic backlog into the Great mall. For the first time in his life, Cisco saw colorful and mighty monuments decorating the gray concrete of the packaging company, no longer just practicality but some culture and a look at the past. Above the workers' dining room stood a huge golden Buddha statue, at the foot of the government offices, cars and carriages were placed in a long line from all times when there were still wide roads to move around. The packaging company was all like a huge museum, a concept that existed only in the university rooms of the Great Mall, like the museum that showcased the development of the mall and the history of Georgio and his ancestors. After an arduous job that lasted for several weeks, Cisco and Subara watched leisurely through the porch of their palace at the museum display they had built and waited for visitors.

Chapter 25

Sunan was not an ordinary child, and since the age of ten, she had found it difficult to adapt to the educational framework of consumerism religion. The source of knowledge she drew from was the news portal, the mall's internal politics attracted her. Only when she was seventeen did she realize that the news edition was dictated from above before she truly believed that this is how the political world of the White Palace was built. Every evening she watched the main news release while her parents and younger siblings played together on "Searching for the Cache" on a virtual solitary island, these were some of the luxuries that families living in the White Palace enjoyed. Her father was a computer manager, giving Sunan access to fascinating information files about history and science. she inherited her mother's expressiveness and wit, working as a marketing woman who ran clothing stores in the northwestern area of the mall. Peeking at the copywriting transcripts her mother composed every night before bedtime, she was inspired to become a reporter later in her adult life. As soon as she graduated at age twenty she was accepted as a correspondent in the "Sacred Broadcasting Division". Some say she was accepted because of her looks and some say it is due to her acquired and innate skills. In any case, years later, she was appointed the chief commentator of the "Mall's Edition" watched by anyone with a chip flowing in his blood. Her subversive thought did not dare to be expressed until that fateful day when she was sent to broadcast an article on the new helmets. Sunan and Fox were told that this is a sacred religious mission ordered by the great Georgio.

The director of broadcasting and communications called them to his office that day, he wanted to talk to them in private: "Georgio himself is worried that the palace workers do not purchase the helmets like the other common mall consumers. So I send you an article that will be broadcast to the chips of the palace employees for the sake of seeing how helmet use is a sacred and blessed commandment. "

"You used a helmet yourself?" Sunan asked her manager about a millisecond later, Fox holding her shoulder, preventing her from continuing to ask. From a very young age, Sunan's doubts arose about the sanctity of the White Palace and Georgio's heavenly control of the big mall, but it was just a feeling and not a really defiant thought.

Her manager frowned and answered her with a rude lie: "Of course, I tried the helmet, well, I haven't tried, but I purchased it and it is placed on my bed for use when I get home. Now go on and try it too and be convincing enough to describe what you experienced." Fox held Sunan's palm and they both walked out of the office straight to the only helmet store in the White Palace.

"Are you ready?" Sunan asked as she sat in front of him holding the helmet over her head while he grabbed the helmet under his armpit. Fox shook his head and they both wore their helmet on their heads as they immediately dived into a virtual reality that felt like a real world. It was only their imagination, Sunan found herself in the mid-20th century A.D in a press office, a time when the paper was inked with a pen. Meanwhile, Fox found himself on a warm beach as he embraced Sunan, she was wearing a minimal swimsuit on her body, and her white skin reddened by the blazing sun rays he had only seen in the movies. Now everything felt so real. When he closed his eyes tightly and concentrated, he managed to touch her helmet and almost lift it, but he liked Sunan's silent and smiling figure. "I probably don't know Sunan enough to say anything in my imaginary world, but I'm comfortable with her being so silent." Fox thought to himself. Sunan got up, held his bare arm, and gave him a warm kiss: "I love you, my Fox." At that moment Fox realized that he never wanted to leave, he and Sunan continued to walk on the beach along its endless length.

Under the helmet in Sunan's world, she had no idea what to do in front of the paper-ejecting typewriter. She saw her office colleagues tapping and typing letters on the pages, she remembered learning how the information had been stored in the past but wasn't sure how to operate the machine. She imitated her peers' actions by tapping on the typewriter buttons, with a jumble of letters that lingered on the page without meaning.

After a few minutes of typing, she turned around behind her, a scowling man, not recognizing her remark: "Why are you wasting paper and ink? I asked you to see the "Source" I told you about."

Sunan replied to the person who appeared to be an authority: "What kind of person are you talking about?"

The authoritative man replied: "That person who promised to give us information about the burglary case has information on the president. He gave an address to meet with him. come on, move it! and don't forget to write down every word. I want a complete article on my desk tomorrow morning."

Sunan rushed over to the exit as her friend pulled her toward the restroom, asking her: "Are you going to meet that "deep throat" you told me about?"

Sunan replied as if she remembered what it was about: "Yes, of course, with a deep throat." She looked in the mirror and saw her friend putting red lotion on her lips. with her and her colleague's body are wearing a physical cloth that blocked all her pores in a way she had never been used to before. She hurried out of her office without her bag and entered the elevator, the only machine she recognized from the White Palace. When she reached the busy street, she looked around and saw how noisy and sooty cars moved, around busy people, some busy with consumerism and some on their other daily missions. It was unclear to Sunan where everyone was in a hurry, but she knew she had to hurry up for the meeting. After asking dozens of people on every corner of the street how to get to the address on the note she was holding in her hand, she finally reached a small, dark alley. As she walked in fear in that alley, a thin palm of a strange hand touched her shoulder causing her to jump with a scream of panic.

"Hello gentle lady, I love how the lipstick is smeared on your lips." Sunan, who didn't know what lipstick was, ignored the disturbing remark even though it still looked good on her lips. As she turned, a tall, sturdy man stood in front of her with a nasty smile and a fedora hat on his head, with his jacket on.

"Are you the deep throat?" Sunan asked as she exhaled in panic.

"I'll let you guess by yourself, move quickly to the next question lady reporter because both of us are running short." The mysterious man bent his back as he turned to look behind him and to his sides and his gaze suddenly became smug to insecure as sweat dripped from his forehead.

A question arose from Sunan's subconscious not understanding where it came from and what context: "Do you know about the president's connection to the office break-in?"

Deep throat replied: "The president is involved in every detail about the burglary, the information stolen in the burglary has helped him greatly in his re-election. His right to be president is therefore in doubt and I as a government employee, must le everyone know that."

Sunan was shocked that a head of state could be unworthy of his own rule, after all, how could anyone who is leading his people be unworthy? Her entire world of concepts was shaken: "I'm afraid I'm a sinner. How can I use this information against my country's leader?" Sunan dropped her little tape recorder as she was confused and anxious. Even so, she didn't know how to use it and what its use was for.

The man put a piece of paper in Sunan's palm, walked away, and said, "The names of those involved in the president's conspiracy are listed. Notice the names closest to him are listed." Sunan dropped the page on the sidewalk but immediately picked it up. As she moved closer to the newspaper's building her dream became more and more faded, the image blurred around her like a fog. She woke up in the white palace with her helmet over her head.

Chapter 26

The packaging company soldiers were infesting the big mall, most of them had already become addicted to using a helmet, every man was preoccupied in his own daydream. The few who were disconnected from it yearned to use it again, which required an extra dollar deposit. They had to ask for a chip connection for payment, thus were no longer governors but instead became Georgio's subjects.

"Sir, the packaging soldiers' annexation has already reached 70%," Intelan informed Georgio who was watching from his Ivory Tower across the Big mall as the mall's tower scraping scratches its baldness. He decided to ignore Intelan's words and take time out in his toddler son's room. The nanny just wiped his milk-smeared mouth. A grin woke up over the toddler when he saw his father approaches him. The nanny walked away and Georgio looked into his eyes without knowing what he should feel about his heir. He raised the baby with both hands and suddenly left one hand to signal a hologram. The hologram content was created at Georgio's command, a tiger running in the jungle seemingly coming towards them, the baby clapping and giggling, then the tiger began to roar loudly and the baby cried for a second. Georgio placed the baby who was in amazement with his eyes wide open, the amused father tapping his finger in the air and the photo changed to a soldier carrying a weapon that would shoot in bundles. The baby shook the coop fearlessly and looked amazed.

Georgio shouted at his son: "Hit him, hit the bad guy!" The baby continued to shake the coop and a minute later he began to cry to the sound of the shots.

The nanny walked cautiously behind Georgio's back and whispered to him: "I smell it, he is crying because he needs to change his diaper." Georgio stopped the hologram as his mind shifted. He quietly walked out of the room and tried to contact Intelan. Georgio noticed that Heinze was lifting the baby, shaking it, and kissing it with great affection to his opinion.

He interrupted the conversation with Intelan and screamed, "Let my son down, you're just the nanny and nothing else." Heinze panicked and the baby dropped from her hands, slid on the pillow, and cried.

"Look what you've done, no wonder you're not a mother yourself." Georgio stared at her with scary and penetrating eyes. She slipped and fell on the floor of the room, shedding tears beside the crying baby. Georgio knelt at her and reached for her as she whimpered. Georgio came out of the room when the silence was enough to disperse. Intelan was waiting for Georgio outside the room, seeing his master approach with a frown, his heart fluttering as his brain processes slowed their turn. Georgio was all upset by his behavior in the presence of his baby, he recalled his father urging him to succeed and excel. His father used to tell him that his purpose is to become a living god, that is why he always had the feeling that he wasn't worthy enough. That feeling has stuck to him to this day and has been pushed deep under his huge ego. Georgio scolded Intelan from the moment he met him, frightened Intelan opened the office door for a meeting he had with Georgio, they both entered the room and he received instructions to reinstall the helmet's software of the hypnotized subjects. Intelan who suffer Georgio's threats continually felt helpless until he let out a shout: "Shut up already!" Intelan who couldn't believe the words coming out of his mouth was silenced. Georgio walked out of the room in a loud silence, Intelan knew his punishment was coming and realized he was expected to be arrested by the police in a matter of minutes. Out of fear and distress, he programmed a malicious code into the helmet terminal to give it external control over the helmet of all residents.

When the police came in with their electrifying batons, he knew he had to atone for his words: "Will you just let me finish my job?" Intelan begged them.

The high-ranking policeman ordered the cops to wait: "You have three seconds to turn off the system and nothing more than that" Intelan turned off the computer and went to the policeman who immediately cuff him,

In his heart, he thought: "The damage has already been done, just hope it is not so visible."

In the dungeon, Intelan was completely disconnected from any means of communication. He was connected only to the chip unilaterally, allowing it to summon information from the system but not communicate and program it for its needs. In the dungeon, he experiences terrible tortures of scary sounds at night. Occasionally, he was hit by a cold or heat stroke, whipping from the guards, and even more, terrifying broadcasts about his life sent to the chip such as messages about his family's death or a painful reminder about deceased loved ones. Intelan thought to himself while physically and mentally tortured: "Nobody knows how to program the helmet as I did, fortunately, I did not cooperate with Georgio. Unfortunately, I will have to cooperate with him so that I will not tolerate further torture. This collaboration will strengthen the brainwashing and hegemony under which Georgio controls the masses." Intelan, who was very realistic, knew that Georgio was not really as special and divine as most of the mall's consumers and employees imagined. What triggered him to obey was the fear of the punishments he received and his questionable future. Georgio watched with pleasure the tortured Intelan, only a few got such a "Georgio style "abuse. Intelan was one of the few who dared to yell at a dominant leader like him and after prolonged brainwashing, there were only a few who dared to confront him. The same rebels never repeated their mistake after the beating of the mall state's owner. Georgio did not abuse Intelan to educate him, it was a sheer pleasure to display his violent power towards someone. After Intelan was no longer able to eat or sleep because of the physical and mental pain he endured, the police picked him up from the prison room and sent him to the White Palace clinic. About a month after completing his sentence and recovering, the engineers saw their chief executive Intelan come into the study with his eyes shut and his back slumped, sad, and less formal than he was used to. Due to his great respect for his wisdom they applauded when he came in, an honor they would not have given him if they knew why he had "fallen asleep" for so long. First, Intelan went to the helmet's main terminal. He sat down and began examining the irreversible malicious code that he had put into the system, a code that would still reveal him as a traitor in Georgio's eyes. At the end of the workday, Intelan headed to a hovercraft adjacent to the engineers' main office, taking off with it south.

Chapter 27

The white palace was sleeping like millions of years old virgin forest, occasionally a rustling sound, palace workers scarcely made some noise. The elevator went up in absolute quiet. Mazda stepped into the tower of the White Palace, it was noisy inside. Before that, she was not authorized to enter that floor. There she hoped she would see Sony, one floor before the top, the Ivory Tower. The thought of Sony made her smile in addition to the belly butterflies, these emotions mixed with anxiety as the elevator door opened. The director of the design division, Appella, waited impatiently for her due to a tight schedule. Mazda hurriedly entered the room without looking right or left out of the fear of being distracted. It took Mazda a few moments to speak.

"Something inside me prevents me from ratting out on people that my subconscious may be identifying with their actions," she thought. At one point, Appella approached her: "Did you come to talk to me about the people who sabotaged our advertising system?"

Mazda stammered a dark woman who was determined to ask more intrusive questions: "Do you have any connection with these people? Are you originally from the packaging company?" These kinds of questions triggered the adrenaline in Mazda that prompted her to respond to Appella's questions: "I managed to follow a group of consumers, it seems That they play a game within the helmet system," Mazda quickly said.

"Through the new helmet system?"Appella questioned, "It is known that the helmet system transmits completely unilaterally and does not receive conscious input from the user."

"Their use of helmets is initial," Mazda replied. "they have been able to penetrate the system through their chip for some time. Through the chip, they reach the intricacies of the White Palace's databases." Appella suspected she might be a double agent, but somewhat she trusted Mazda that was innocently drifted into contact with this gang and could use her to stop them.

Appella began by saying, "I know you can contact this group, so I recommend that you be promoted to the position of Information Security Manager. Your job will be to secure the content we produce in the advertising industry."

Mazda hesitated for a moment: "I would be more than happy to be promoted to this position, but I'd rather sleep on it. It's a role with a very big responsibility for an inexperienced like me."

Appella interrupted Mazda's remarks: "We both know that this job is way over your head, but I will make sure you get to work one floor above me, upstairs, with all the benefits, close to holiness in the highest possible way."

"You know I'm a simple girl from the packaging company, I haven't been educated on the sacred and religious values, I just came here to make a living," Mazda said as she stood on her trembling legs as she left the room. As she walked down the hall to her amazement, she saw a long entourage pass by, including Sony, covered in a shimmering coat. She could easily identify his sunglasses-wearing face. As the entourage passed, Sony bowed his head so no one could recognize him, from the force of habit. Mazda wanted to return to Appella's room and tell her that she agreed to the coveted job on the floor where Sony worked, but unfortunately, the elevator was already going down on its way to the bottom of the White Palace tower.

The next morning, Mazda woke up with the decision to leave her life as a junior saleswoman behind and move on to a more fulfilling life. She imagined herself holding Sony's hands, walking through the corridors of the White Palace while everyone is cheering while loud music is playing in the background, with many applause and confetti in the air. When she awoke from her daydream in her bed, wandered around in her mind, she knew that the chip absorbed her feelings of indecision and dilemma so she tried as little as possible to think about what was bothering her. When she tried to change her mind about her family and childhood, she preferred to go back to thinking about her new career, which again raised thoughts of indecision that she preferred to avoid. If she tried to think of Sony, he reminded her that she was going to work upstairs next to him, and then thoughts began again like, "Should I leave the job that I love and enjoy or should I move toward an office alongside Sony." She tried to avoid the thought, to close her eyes that were not really tired, and to go back to sleep. Due to the reluctance of Mazda's body to go back to sleep, she looked at the helmet that lay next to her bed, a helmet she had received for the purpose of customer demonstration and had to keep. She never wore a helmet on her head except for a demo. She avoided using a helmet after seeing on the streets of the mall how addictive and devastating it was. Despite the fear, she chose to flee into the shadow of the helmet world. She realized these were the thoughts she wanted to get in front of anyone who might be listening to her dilemmas, even though she told her new boss: "I have to think about it." She knew that the White Palace did not take no for an answer especially it was such a generous offer. She knew she lived in an age when thoughts were common ground. Mazda screened the most flattering hologram dress that showed professionalism and authority, she had a great selection of dresses from her work in the White Palace. She went up for the second time to the top floor of the palace's human resources manager, this time even more stressed.

"I decided to accept Appella's proposal." Said Mazda to Manpowerena with a fake smile on her face. "Manpowerena answered with a genuine smile:" I'm glad to hear, dear Mazda, I hope you start vigorously today, your tasks will be supervising the analyst's crew operations at the mall and investigating the hacking attempts to the palace. " She knew where to start, going back to the mall and locating Helmet # 243 that was held by the burglars, she knew that the only card that gave her an advantage in getting the job was the very fact that the burglars were holding Helmet 243, so she kept that information secret, which gave her an exclusive advantage in locating the gang. Mazda entered the information security room, where staff members were waiting for her on, the top floor, which received her with applause, smiles, and cheering, Mazda did not suspect for a moment that she was carefully appointed and that her recruitment was not accidental.

Chapter 28

Intelan has crossed the border between the Big mall and the packaging company, a short walking route but a long and strenuous mental journey to hack his chip. He managed to walk a few steps and passed the two guards at the entrance to the company grounds. To his delight, he did not stop by them and continued to walk towards the gray buildings, a shapeless appearance and lacking the sense of aesthetics he had grown accustomed to it from the White Palace. So what is he facing? Will he seek asylum? From every corner, there was an impressive and large monument, whether it was a weather balloon, a diminutive model of pyramids, etc. Around each monument stood some curious people who spent their time reading the plaque placed by Subara, teaching about the object in front of their eyes. Intelan read the inscription under a huge device that caught his eye, four by four metal squares standing one on top of the other and with a glass window, the sign says: "Laundry machine from the late 20th century, appliances that clean people's clothing." Intelan did not understand how to clean human clothing and recalled that his chief technician's uniform hologram had to be changed to a blue-gray uniform so as not to stand out from the packaging companies crowd, and so he did with the help of the chip was not connected to the mall state's intranet anymore and was exclusively under his own control. He moved toward the entrance of a tall building that its guards were with a serious countenance, their red eyes constantly looking to the sides as he approached them, sniffing him thoroughly. When he just started to say, "How can I..." immediately caught by them, they pulled him in forcibly into the building. Intelan was put in a small room with no windows when the soldier sat him down on a chair and grabbed both of his hands to his back. The female soldier said: "You smell like a pure human, you are from the big mall! I'm sure I don't need you to answer this question."

Intelan reacted puzzled as he groaned from the soldier's arms: "How did you find out that my chip did not belong to the packaging company?"

The soldier answered him abruptly: "I am the one who is asking the questions now. We have no chips but we can identify strangers through our sense of smell without intravenous means." The soldier smiled at Intelan and asked, "Why did you come in here? What is your role at the Big mall?"

Intelan decided not to hide his identity and replied to the other soldier: "I have a very senior position in the White Palace, a specialist in networks and computers. I can be of great help to you."

The soldier turned and thought for a moment: "If you are so senior then how come you are so easily caught, it's like you wanted to be caught? How would I know if you are not a double agent?"

The soldier bent intelan's arm more intently and was about to bite him when mucus ran out of his mouth: "I didn't mean ..." Intelan groaned in pain and continued to murmur: "I just ran away ..." The female soldier looked at Intelan with his poor eyes and ordered her colleague to stop his painful action.

"Come on," she told Intelan, "go with me to our engineering department." The female soldier thought at her heart as Intelan tried to get out of his chair: "Maybe I can go back to my previous job as an engineer if I bring this kind of human resource of such value to the department!"

"What is your name?" she was Asked by Intelan as he tried to connect to the packaging company's digital intranet, he was surprised that he felt more passionate about knowing her name than to hack the packaging company system.

"My name is Ika," she replied as she examined his actions in front of the computer. He felt she was watching as he coded against the hologram presentation that gave him highly classified information. He had never felt so special to a girl, the first time someone noticed him and smiled at him. Intelan had no idea what to do in front of a shapely young woman who looks at him like this, wearing a real, tight military uniform. Her features resembled a watchdog's face, but her human beauty was still evident. He did not feel particularly attractive in his slender, low-cut appearance, clad in the hologram-free gray suit he was used to wearing when he was at the White Palace.

A few days after she capture Intelan, Ika was accepted as a network engineer for a trial period while she supervised Intelan's work under her role as guardian. As she watched him, Ika was marveled at his simple and ordinary human look without any gene additions. Indeed, she made sure to provide him raw food with no gene supplements, but she did want to ask for permission to stop being fed with the pitbull gene supplement she received and instead to be given the owl-dolphin gene supplement again, as owls and dolphins are known to have no fewer brain functions than humans, which can help a packaging company engineer to have a better perspective. Something about her heart did not allow her to change Intelan, she loved his human appearance as it was.

One day she woke up to the sound of his question: "Tell me Ika, do you keep me from escaping or do you oversee the work I do?"

Ika smiled when she heard his question and thought about it lightly before answering: "Neither this nor that, now that they have received me back as an engineer, I will try to get back to my engineering skills, I would rather be near you with curiosity and not with the necessity of keeping you." Ika went on as Intelan listened to her as he dove into her round gray eyes that momentarily lost their puppy eyes as she said: "I would have preferred to be more productive and less in a combative position, I think that is how I contribute better to the packaging company."

Intelan replied: "But is that what you were born to do? Is it the fate and natural talent that lies in you?" Intelan who used to think in the mall's way of thinking only saw people with a special talent, geniuses born to serve masters. Ika replied: "I was born a blank page like all my friends, all of us in the packaging company are equal, our qualities we acquire here is for the benefit of the collective." Ika was impressed by the deep questions asked by Intelan, his innovative form of thought provoked affection in her. Intelan, unaccustomed to receiving affection from the opposite sex, could not interpret the codes that came to his eyes and tickled him under his nose. He sank back into his virtual mission where he continued to hack the scripts of the Big mall helmets to accomplish his big, secret plan.

160

"What are you doing there?" Ika turned to him as she lightly patted his shoulder and smiled at him again, "I hope you can break into the big mall's computer."

Intelan cynically replied to her: "I notice that you are programming the packaging company stencils."

Ika, on the other hand, saw it as a naughty wink: "You're right," Ika smirked, "I do my routine and boring maintenance programming, while you are breaking into a fascinating new world. I wish I could rise above the usual instructions." Ika couldn't help it, she got up and kissed Intelan on his cheek, he grabbed her and kissed her on the lips in front of the other surprised engineers. Ika felt embarrassed that her authority and responsibility for Intelan was undermined, though she loved the courageous and spontaneous act that Intelan had preform. Unfortunately for Intelan, he was repulsed by Ika's great power that hit him on the floor, she still had the muscle strength of an average pitbull. In a fraction of a second, they both sat down, like nothing had happened on their chairs, and continued their work, this time without talking for long hours. After her embarrassment expires from her heart, she couldn't stop herself from asking Intelan: "How come you are able to hack these inner contents so easily? Obviously, it's not your high cognitive ability, so what allows you to concentrate for such a long time despite your human limitations?"

Intelan replied: "I've never been strong in the real world, I perform better in virtual worlds." He continued: "When I write code, I allow myself to go over every possible law. A good writer must break the law in his writing."

Ika did not understand what he was talking about and asked: "Shouldn't you follow the rules in order for you to break through the system?", Intelan replied "On the contrary, I have to break every possible rule and law in order to succeed. In the real world, I have only broken the law once. And unfortunately, I paid a heavy price for it, again it was when I kissed you. It was the second courageous act of my life. " Ika was muted with another embarrassment that landed on her and both turned their heads to the hologram's projections and returned to their work.

Chapter 29

"The elite is in control of the means of production, and the working class has the power of production itself," Gogol recalled in a quote from a philosopher from the past. "But what about who has both the means and the production power of the nanobots?" Gogol thought as he sat alone on his sofa And went on to reflect: "Anyone who controls nanobots controls all right of existence and is the only class, everything else exists only in his right." Gogol came up with the idea that the chip-making and helmets were made exclusively by the Georgio-controlled nanobots, they couldn't be controlled by Intelan or its subordinate engineers. As he pondered and walked around in unrest, he noticed how the void inside the room symbolized for him the loneliness that had resulted from his wife's absence. From his apartment, Gogol went down to the cafe to try to get an idea of how he could influence the nanorobotic helmet production process. Maybe this way he can bring back his wife who was trapped with her head inside a helmet. He met up with his co-workers at the "Career Cafe" on the first entertainment floor in front of the White Palace gate, where he thought he would share his sad feelings. One of the people sitting next to him at the coffee table was Magimix, the chief marketing executive of the big mall. Gogol knew that any emotion that would spill from his heart to Magimix's ears may be used against him someday.

Every now and then, smiling girls passed by as they looked at Gogol who was a tall man and oozed charisma with his fake smile. Gogol continued to smile despite feeling as though the world was about to collapse. As his friends talked to each other, he realized that it is impossible to manage a perfect career and a love life at the same time, must give up something along the way. His friends preferred not to ask him about his shaky marital status, even though they knew he was in a rather lost and lonely place in his personal life. Gogol closed his eyes and returned to the moment when Georgio adopted him as a child from a devastated family. Any family in the big mall can be considered devastated in that respect, but no family member in the big mall felt that way. Gogol's family was not originally from the big mall and Gogol had a very murky memory of them. Gogol recalled his childhood the moment Georgio looked at him as a speechwriter as part of a speech-writing competition. Hundreds of children were invited to the competition in the ballroom to serve in the White Palace. Gogol had trouble remembering what happened before the moment when Georgio had taken him.

"Gogol wake up!" Magimix Giggled at him as he shook his shoulder.

"Do you remember moments from your early childhood, Magimix?" Gogol abruptly asked when the other members of the conversation, including Georgio's chief technician and secretary, burst out laughing at the surprising question. Magimix was surprised by the question and shared how he played in the White Palace nursery, how he was raised by his father and mother, and shared some memories from his third birthday and more.

Gogol turned to Worda the secretary: "You have little kids, right?"

The secretary nodded, "I'm sure they remember early moments in their lives."

Worda didn't know what to answer and Gogol wondered in a loud voice that everyone can hear as he looked up at the nanobots hovering like dust on their heads: "I don't understand why I don't have childhood memories."

MagiMix answered with a wink: "I guess you run out of memory space of fascinating memories on your chip in your blood." Magimix laughed and so did the rest of the group.

"What does this have to do with a chip?" Gogol asked him in a tense voice as he shook his body with both hands.

"Relax, I am just kidding."

"No, you didn't laugh with me" Gogol got up and continued on his way. "Something about the chip inside me keeps me from remembering." Gogol pressed and decided to go up to the chip manufacturer floor, perhaps where he would understand what he was talking about. Gogol knew that Magimix was just kidding, but there might be something in the chip that helps Georgio control his personal and other people's collective memory. Gogol was never intrigued to check the contents of his chip, he completely relied on the communications system in the big mall and did not suspect anything. Ever since his wife became addicted to using a helmet, something about his confidence has cracked.

After arriving at the large chip development experimental lab, he went to the main development computer. Gogol put his hands in the chipmaker's main computer. He tried to produce a chip replacement but with no success. He wanted to get his chip out of his body, but The odds were against him for the chip being traced and caught by the system out of all the gallons of blood in his body. He would have to locate the chip digitally and read it, but how could he do that? Gogol wanted to consult with Intelan but he wasn't around. Deciding to take on a new approach and find someone who would try to work with a brand new blank chip, Gogol opened the chipset system to create a new chip. But he saw nothing but voice, picture, and conversation transfer functions. As if the chips were just for communication and have no content of their own or mind control instructions as he suspected. The chip manufacturing engineers gave Gogol access to their workplace without interruption, they thought he was sent from above as a supervisor reviewer.

The chip's chief production manager approached Gogol: "Can I help you in some way?"

Gogol asked her, "tell me, is it possible to program the chip to control the brain?"

The manager was taken aback by the question and answered him: "Not at all, the chip is only intended to transmit information directly to the brain without the senses of the body, but it cannot dictate to the brain how to interpret them."

Gogol replied: "But if the chip can show information to the brain, can't it prevent the brain from remembering certain things?" The manager stammered in amazement: "I am appalled by the question. I can't believe the chip is capable of ..."

Gogol interrupted: " You Do know that the chip is capable, it presents directly to consciousness, maybe it can prevent consciousness from certain thoughts?"

167

The manager nodded: "In principle yes if he is able to transmit information from outside to the virtual reality helmet he can also affect the recall process even without a helmet."

"Then you admit it is possible," Gogol pointed his finger at her, and went out the entrance of the chip manufacturing lab, leaving the wide-open mouth manager by herself and quickly disappeared.

Chapter 30

"You will have to resign in public," Gogol told Peugeot in a private conversation. Peugeot's eyes were lowered down as he sat in his executive chair, playing with the buttons of his virtual shirt.

"After the physical threat of the invading soldiers is over, do you take away the highest-ranking job I've ever achieved?" Peugeot answered with a wailing tone.

Gogol approached Peugeot's desk and said weakly to him: "You must take responsibility for this omission, your police officers have been unable to prevent the invasion."

Peugeot interrupted: "So now you will choose a new prime minister and throw me out on the streets?"

Gogol shook his head as he moved away to the window: "You have to understand that we will take care of you, you will be our consultant in the White Palace. Georgio assured you. He trusts for

Peugeot got up from his chair and said, "I'm tired of you, I'm the ruler of the mall. The People elected me and I will reveal your method."

Gogol laughed and answered him calmly: "Do you really think you ever dominated or elected?"

Peugeot sat back in his chair and turned it toward the wide window that looked out into the depths of the Big mall: "If I ask you for a personal favor, leave me on this chair for a while so I can find a fairer way to quit."

Gogol replied without flinching: "And what can Mr. Prime Minister give me in return? You didn't think I'd do anything against the interest of the company just like that."

"I can give you every possible bit of information about your big boss, who I'm not afraid of and never saw as a god on earth, despite my attempts to portray him as such in the eyes of the population," Peugeot answered him as he turned to Gogol with a nasty smile. Gogol felt a tremor in his body by the reminder that his boss was nothing but flesh and blood. The internalization that Georgeo is not almighty cause him to shiver and a drop of sweat trickled down his face as he answered Peugeot: "If only some reminder or even a hint of his control of my memory is found, I'm sure you have censorship control archives that you shed."

Peugeot was taken aback by Gogol's frightened look and answered: "You will need to access the files that I will bring

you to the company's information security system, from the system in the White Palace you will be able to decode these files. Accompany my assistant Coca to the review that she will do. She will have to come for further inspection "
"no one should know That I will suddenly appear alongside the company's new information security manager. "

Gogol was referring to a Mazda whose name had slipped from his memory, the next day Mazda learned of an important meeting with the mall's chief censor to check information files in the main archive. She was told to be present.

"Hello, Chief Censor," she stammered with insecurity so unworthy of her role.

Coca gowned in a puffy red dress with purple murmurs whispered to Mazda: "Let's finish this hassle as soon as possible, I haven't yet seen such a beautiful manager like you" Mazda blushed for a moment, then felt the weight of the role on her shoulders. She was in no way allowed to let anyone access the main archive alone, only she and automatic nanobots were allowed to extract files. While Coca was browsing the archives, Gogol suddenly entered with his hands clasped in the back as he was holding a memory card in his palm.

From her lack of political understanding, she block Gogol's passage, which made him angry: "Are you ready to leave?" Gogol scolded her.

Mazda was dreading to lose her job but did not know Gogol as she scolded him back: "Why are you talking to me like that? Because of my young age or because I am a woman? I have achieved this role honestly."

Coca chuckled and said to Mazda: "Darling, you know this is Georgio's chief advisor. If you want to keep your position, open I suggest you leave the room or.." Then Coca whispered in her ear: "At least look at his actions with one eye open from the outside. "Coca continued the routine work of running applications in the White Palace system as if she would find anything bad she would report it, but everything Coca did was essentially technical without any special attention to the content that was revealed to her. Gogol came in when Mazda got nervous on her way out of the room with her head down, not knowing whether to get angry or scold herself for her mistake. While running the edited file that Peugeot gave him, Gogol went through the lists in the file until he came across one called: "Nanobotic Programmable Protocol Chip". Gogol opened the protocol while Mazda couldn't decide whether to keep an eye on Coca or Gogol. Gogol reviewed the protocols and discovered a function that opens a chip and implements visual "long-term memory" information. Gogol discovered the possibility that someone was erasing his childhood memories with the chip in his mind. He deleted all the information except the "memory transplant" function and went with quick steps and a poker face out of the room after which Coca greeted Mazda goodbye. Mazda, in her curiosity, checked Gogol's hub connection point and saw exactly what Gogol opened, Category: "Chip Programming Protocol", Subcategory: "Long-term dummy memory implantation". Mazda was shocked. Her understanding of the possibility of chip programming by an external factor has seriously hampered the security of residents in the mall, leaving the archive room as she thought of ways to stop the hackers who hacked the helmets. "If they knew how to break into the chips and people's memory they could control the entire mall." Mazda, in her lack of understanding, thought that breaking into a chip as possible from the outside, what motivated her was her fear and lack of technical knowledge. She assumed the chip could be hacked like the helmets. Gogol, however, was furious. He tried to contact Intelan again, but he was long out of the reach of all the members of the big mall and the White Palace. Gogol, after an unsuccessful attempt to locate Intelan, decided to consult a computer specialist at the White Palace Academy.

Chapter 31

The streets of the mall were filled with shoppers dressed in colorful clothes following the annual "consumer holiday". Every morning, entire families emerged from their sleeping capsules, but this morning, holograms were dazzled with bright colors and particularly glowing intensely, dancing to the sounds of loud electronic music echoing throughout the mall. Among the sounds, Mazda heard them sing:

" We are the rulers, the consumer class!

The workers below us are locked in the palace.

If you do not buy, pack more cargo,

The packaging company never dares.

Georgio watches out that the government will not budge.

The mall is for us workers, wake up! "

174

Mazda did not understand how it was that consumers did not recognize their sad state of affairs, as far as she was concerned, a symbol of a kind of futile future. As she walked within the celebrating and joyous crowd, It dawned on her, that apparently she had been living an erroneous pursuit of career and achievements. The Volksfugan family with their three children flew holograms of inflatable balloons up into the mall space, the parents created the balloons in a multitude of colors and the children hit them and flung them up. Mazda who danced with the crowd and changed dresses in colors and decorations came across this family. As she looked at them, a flash of memory of her family, father, mother, and little brother came to her mind. Everyone huddles in the audience, looking at the background, and then her memory was cut off.

The father of the Volksfugan family approached her and asked: "Young maid, want to hold a balloon?"

Mazda replied with instinct: "How much does it cost?"

"It's a gift, I wouldn't dishonor myself in a sales job," the father and his wife chuckled: "Don't you know that people of our class are not allowed to do any work? We are meant to buy and enjoy, this is the mall's good world."

Mazda addressed the mother in a critical tone: "Wouldn't you rather your father's children support you and improve your life?" the mother saw Mazda's dress hologram disappear and become a work suit. She officially returned to the position of security manager in search of the hacker gang before they could do damage to the White Palace again.

"Why did you take away your beautiful dress?" The father of the family asked with a flushed face and took an elbow in his chubby stomach from his wife who grimaced her jealous face.

Mazda replied: "I see no reason to celebrate your miserable situation, instead we strive together for a better life for you and your children."

The mother burst into her: "We will not do any work, instead we live, have fun and buy," that is what Georgio said, he wants us to enrich our shopping cart and prosper, As it is written..."

Mazda answered her with an angry tone as her cheeks went red: "If Georgio really cares about you then why do we workers have better and more comfortable luxuries?"

The older daughter intervened for the sake of her mother and sounded recited: "Georgio would like US to rest and for YOU to be slaves and so he compensates you for the agony of your souls. That's what we learned in the educational broadcast."

Mazda leaned over to the girl and said: "From where I came from, everyone cares for each other and everyone is equal, Georgio cares only for himself ..."
Suddenly Mazda paused for a few seconds and she was hit by a strong electric current in her head, after she felt a severe migraine, before she even finished the sentence. The stunned father repeated: "Does Georgio only care for himself?" And suddenly he had a severe migraine. The girls of the Volksfugan family giggled and said without even thinking about the consequences: "Georgio cares only for himself" and also grabbed a headache that flung them to the floor to the amazement of the mother who thought: "I must never say such a sentence, I must think of something else", She carried her children and dragged the dizzy and stunned father as they left her handbag behind. Mazda came up with an idea that it might be best to wear the beautiful dress that Mr. Volksfugan recommended. It's better to look attractive as the manager of the security company.

On the store sign "Hologram Repair Lab" lights flashed, a satisfied customer walked out of the store in her flashing dress as Mazda came in. One of the shop's technicians allowed her in, to the best of Mazda's memory, it was one of Rayban's band. She noticed Rayban and put her hand on his shoulder with a smile. It took Rayban a few seconds to take his busy look away from the monitor and direct it to Mazda. He was fascinated by her beauty and cascading hair, her bright, slender face, and her reddish-pink cut in the hologram dress she wore.

"Haven't you got to Sony yet?"Rayban asked contemptuously.

Mazda felt that he craved her and utilized every bit of energy in her body to influence him. "I decided I wanted to spend more time with you. I'm tired of working for the White Palace all day."

Rayban replied: "You know I'm also a White Palace employee, I fix holograms."

Mazda nodded: "So how come you are opposed to using helmets and producing so many riots instead of just having fun?".Rayban turned his head again and replied, "I haven't known anyone fun like you yet." He touched her palm and tried to wiggle his fingers with her fingers but she pulled him from the chair towards a more inner room in front of his astonished friends. Mazda and Rayban passionately kissed from the moment the door slammed until they lay on a couch under a virtual window. Mazda stopped the lovemaking and

178

asked: "Have you ever tried to say something against Georgio or the Big mall?",

"If I tried to say something about Georgio loudly, I would have experienced a very severe physical injury. I don't know if you tried to do that, but as the residents of the mall, we refrain from resisting. It may be a brainwash we have had since childhood or it is due to something else."

"Something else?" Mazda looked directly into Rayban's eyes and waited for an answer,

Rayban answered her with a hesitant, stuttering tone: "It's just a theory but I think it's something about the chips, that's why I try to break into them. For a long time, we've been trying to find proof that the chips..." Suddenly, Rayban choked and fainted, his mouth opening and his eyeballs whitening. Mazda tried to open the window and out of the room but found out that it had no exit but only an outside view covering the wall. She managed to run away, with no choice, shouting: "Rescue! He suddenly crashed. I swear I have no idea how." Tears streamed down her face as her heart pounded hard. One of his friends ran to check Rayban who was lying on the floor while two others clutched at Mazda on both sides of her body in rage. "That's not me!" Mazda screamed as she sank to her feet as they walked her out of the store.

Chapter 32

Subara cut the ribbon at the unveiling ceremony while standing above an archaeological exhibit outside the mall. The crowd rallied and applauded, the human dogs barked and clapped, the bat of like men waving their winged hands. A growing crowd of immigrants from the Big mall has been exposed to interesting cultural attractions. Every immigrant who came from the mall state underwent an electromagnetic scan to destroy the chip in his body, so the new residents could be exposed to the culture of the packaging company and be integrated into it. The ceremony was covered by journalist Sunan and her companion Fox, both of whom were allowed to survey the art palace on behalf of the White Palace to show the degeneracy and hedonism in which the packaging company suffered. Sunan spoke into Fox's camera with her back facing the performance. The performance was a 20th-century Maserati race car whose wheels turned toward the glass ceiling of the Big mall. Sunan turned her head to read the inscription on the copper sign by the packaging company: "A statue depicting man's desire to reach the stars, at that time was the ambition of mankind to set up a home and a pleasant iron-clad head" (which was actually the car chassis). Alongside a thriving industry, "(what was actually the parts of the hood)" and above as you can see the four major planets, a sculpture by Maserati. " Sunan remained silent and looked at Subara in her speech: "Maserati expressed every man's dreams at that time, he did not know what a shocking end would fall on humanity as it all lusted for consumerism and idolatry. We, The hybrids, know how to dilute the dangerous human power by creating a planned society that its members are Engineered. " Sunan turned her head and exclaimed at the camera excitedly: "So we see another propaganda by the packaging company leader who is supposed to excite the masses and suppress their minds. They are known for their use of chemicals to wash their people's minds, but we are witnessing another manipulation of a confident artist. " Sunan concluded her words as Fox smiled, admiring her beauty and wisdom. The convention moved to the main building, which allowed Sunan and Fox to approach and report about the ancient sculpture.

Fox looked at the statue and smirked: "It looks like part of an upside-down train cart."

Sunan punched him in the shoulder: "You and your imagination and exuberance, now come and photograph me in front of the statue." Sunan read from a hologram teleprompter projected from Fox's camera: "Great Georgio would not allow such an abominable statue to express one man's feelings against the bonds of society, the White Palace reporter said". Sunan did not understand the logic of the sentence: "How could Georgio forbid it?" Sunan said aloud to the camera. She added: "If Georgio does not allow the expression of such a statue, he probably does not have much confidence in his faith." Fox turned the camera off in panic after hearing Sunan's words. Sunan did not understand why these words Slip of the tongue was lurking in the middle of a broadcast and how dare she think of Georgio like that, but a sigh of relief was emanating from her. Shocked and angry, the thought arose that a certain force in the packaging company was causing her these forbidden ideas. Sunan dragged Fox toward the Central Nation Hall where the packaging company executives gathered. As they entered the hall, they saw hordes of strange people like dog men guarding the entrance and watching over Subara standing on the stage. In addition, there were sharp-eyed owls with brown puffy hair around them. The men and women of the harsh ants and bees were also brought in there as the workers' representatives to hear what Subara the queen had to say, and other genetic hybrids that stunned Sunan until she instructed Fox to continue filming the event. At this event, thousands of people gathered in a huge hall eating at tables loaded with engineered food trays. Each group of people according to their function ate from a table on which they were allowed to eat a specifically engineered food. Sunan, unaware of the food features, sampled delicious gourmet dishes that caught her eye. The foods seemed very innocent like grilled chicken, spectacular and varied salads, whipped cream cakes, and pastries of various kinds.

Fox stopped Sunan and tried to explain to her that this food was fully processed, he whispered to Sunan in her ear: "Honey, you have to understand that the food the is being served here is very different from what we are served in the White Palace, it is worse than the pills that spread throughout the big mall."

"What makes you think so?" Sunan answered him with a whisper that helped him feel the warmth of her body.

"In my opinion, this food affects the subjects of this society, that's what makes them what they are, it explains the chemical sensation in the tongue," he told her.

Sunan pulled Fox in his arm, running amok toward the main stage: "Open the microphone, I want everyone to hear" shouted Sunan. Subara allowed her guards to raise Sunan to the stage as she stood out in her human appearance among the crowd.

"I want to ask you, Madam, are you influencing your subjects through transgenic food to hate Georgio and the mall state?" Sunan waited for an answer as she gasped, she couldn't put the question better.

Subara cautiously asked her: "Madam correspondent, how did you come to this conclusion?"

Sunan answered without hesitation: "It seems to me that the food I tasted here made me think wrongly against Georgio, the business leader of the White Palace and the owner of the mall you are a part of."

"It seems that if you had any false thoughts against your boss, you would not be so frightened. On the contrary, he seems you have been purging heresy while you are outside his area of control." Sunan felt humiliated with the audible laughter, while the security guards were giggling along with the crowd and removed their arms from Sunan and Fox. They left the hall on their own with a sense of humiliation and confusion.

Sunan told the stunned Fox: "I want to go and interview Georgio himself, why should he ban the artistic publication of this kind of sculptures?" Fox was stunned and nodded in agreement. They picked up their belongings and after an hour of traveling by a packaging company train, they exited the secure entrance gate into the Big mall not before one of the mall's police guards injected a chip that immediately ran in their blood. When Sunan and Fox appeared at the White Palace gates, the mission for which they came had already been forgotten.

Chapter 33

Gogol's only excuse to approach a college professor without Georgio suspecting him was to come on a review tour. More specifically, Gogol was frightened and excited even when he arrived at the college the comptroller on behalf of the company. It was a special visit, one that gathered more respect around him than a visit by a president of a country. Indeed, As Gogol came to the entrance of the college he was accepted with honor only kings get, and kings have already long gone and passed away from the world and all that remains is one king who finances and takes care of the preservation of the Academy. All the researchers were there at the Gogol hospitality ceremony, from the dean to the last lecturer. They even got to bounce some students from their home who showed great motivation for the White Palace ambassador. Gogol tried to shorten the ceremony to access the most important faculty at the entrance of the building, the Faculty of Economics and Marketing. Professor Salesforce invited him to look at the work of one of his best minds, they walked toward the research wing, each researcher sitting in front of his hologram screen, computing and writing formulas that were beyond Gogol's grasp.

The professor introduced one of his trainees to Gogol: "This is a very senior doctor of mine. He is responsible for the highest analysis of all economic structure statistics, both of the packaging company and of the Big mall."

Gogol commented to Professor Salesforce: "You probably mean the White Palace versus the packaging company. They are all part of the big mall owned by Georgio." Gogol had to make this correction even though all that went through his mind was how to get out of there and get to a microchip and computers expert. To his surprise, Coca came in, patted Gogol's high shoulder, and said: "Sorry for being late, your honor. Professor, you have to finish, the delegation must continue the tour towards the next faculties in line." Gogol breathed with relief and was about to head to the Faculty of Computer Science when Coca stopped him: "Now we go down to the ground floor at the Faculty of Life Sciences."

One of Salesforce's researchers got up from her chair and approached Coca, bowing her head: "My Honorable Lady, my name is Parable, I would love to present you with the results of a socio-political study that will be of great interest to you."

Salesforce interrupted: "I'm sure the delegation has more important things to do." Parable bowed her head again and returned to her work position. Gogol pushed Coca toward the exit, hoping they could continue their day. Coca smiled at him, but he was very stressed and frustrated that she accompanied him.

In the "Faculty of Life Sciences and Human Medicine," they seemed to be facing a team of researchers deeply immersed in tests and less in Human relations. Gogol stood aside as Coca approached a professor who was looking at a hologram of intracellular photography. The lab assistant presented her with a glass plate that contained a specimen, Professor Pfizera turned with the glass in her hand and introduced it directly to Gogol and Coca: "Here is the specimen that will change the world's balance of power, biological nanobots!" Pfizera said, leaving no room for mystery.

Gogol answered her with a dismissive tone: "Is it not problematic to use biological nanobots when they are living or growing outside the human body?"

The professor replied to him while the lab assistant behind her twisted his face to Gogol's question: "I think you are right, to date non-biological nanobots have introduced advanced aviation and survivability capabilities in all weather conditions and atmospheres, as opposed to biological ones that survived only in the biological medium" Coca got tired of the scientific conversation and started walking around the lab in search of eye-catching samples.

Professor Pfizera continued: "In this piece of glass there is a prototype that we have developed through genetic tests on spores, experiments that can give us a real competitive possibility of biological nanobots against ordinary ones."

Gogol shook his head with great interest: "Madam, how long do you think we can produce an efficient and good amount of this kind of nanobots controlled by a biological computer?" Pfizera shook her head awkwardly, in that split second, Gogol's nose smelled of a strange smell emanating from the microorganism-filled tubes. Gogol, like all the residents of the big mall, never breathed outside air and never dazzled with the sun's heat. For the first time, it flooded him with the feeling that it was beyond the air conditioners and flashlights. It brought back memories of ancient worlds he had studied at the White Palace school. The smell reminded him of prehistoric swamp holograms that had been shown to him at school.

At that moment, Professor Pfizera answered his question: "I am convinced that in the near future we will be able to introduce you to a working prototype," Coca picked up a test tube and asked: "What is this fragrant test tube?" Gogol removed the test tube from Coca and led her out as he greeted the research team: "I thank you all, we were very impressed with the visit." At the request of Coca, the last stop they had to pass was the Faculty of Humanities and History. Professor

188

Britanik was immersed in an old prototype of the well-known and marketed helmet that was sold throughout the Big mall. Gogol tapped his fingers on his helmet, drawing the attention of the professor who seemed to get up from his sleep, yawned and congratulated Gogol: "What distinguished guests like you are doing in my dusty office?"

Coca was quick to answer: "We are reviewing on behalf of the Academy Donation System, whether the donations are legal and effective..."

Gogol continued with Coca's remarks: "With your permission, we just want to quickly review the syllabus and the research content you have accumulated, just to check that there is no prohibited material from the pre-mall period." Gogol was referring to the period before the Big mall, the official narrative was that the Big mall was spread across the entire earth, a narrative that led to the closing of the Department of Astronomy and Geology that differed from that argument. Professor Britnik rushed to the central database at the end of the room pulled out old information cards and put them in his pocket.

"I'm just refreshing the software and converting the files to a current version, for decades no one has visited me here."

"Don't bother converting any cards professor, we're in a hurry," Coca realized the professor was trying to hide prohibited information, but Gogol who rushed to visit the computer science faculty pulled Coca out of the room.

Gogol said goodbye to Coca, and separate himself from the tour to meet with the head of the computer science faculty. "On second thought, we will meet in a neutral place in the college cafeteria." Gogol broadcast to Professor Qualcomizaki. Gogol went straight to the point: "I did not come to visit you on financial matters but to ask a simple question" The surprised professor who did not know why he met such a senior personality in a location where full-time students meet after a lecture, listened patiently and with a loud silence. Gogol continued: "You probably know a command called:" Long term memory transmission. "Gogol introduced Professor Qualcomizaki to the function he found on the white palace servers. The professor looked at it reluctantly:" This function can be written into a chip, this chip is powered by an external server And it is not hackable, not by me anyway. I might as well be controlled by the chip in my head myself, even though I have the knowledge to break it, I can't control the chip. "Gogol stopped the professor, stood up, and then turned around and said," So you admit there is a possibility of controlling human memory. "The professor nodded slightly out of fear. Gogol continued on his way.

190

Chapter 34

Ika asked Intelan while sitting in front of his console: "Why are you tirelessly trying to break into the packaging company database?"

Intelan answered her while ticking at the hologram virtual keyboard projected under his fingers: "If I can prove breaches in the repository, I can present them to your queen and she in return will allow me to work as her security expert, ensuring us a good future here, together."

Ika smirked as she stroked her lover's hair: "You don't have to improve your life in the packaging company. Everyone here is enjoying an equal life in every role. We are always being taken care of and we are always safe." Intelan ignored Ika's words and kept ticking until a discovery in cyberspace caught his attention and he remained frozen to Ika's curiosity.

"I think I discovered a breach in the White Palace security system." Intelan said decisively as he cut the thread of Ika's thought: "It could be of great help to you, if you want to go back to work for your master in the White Palace and find out about this loophole, you will be considered a hero!"

Intelan looked at Ika: "I'm too scared to go back and confront him. I think you're braver than me, the one who physically fights and protects your home. I'm just hiding behind the desktop."

But she quickly replied: "I'm really not brave, when I heard that our soldiers had disappeared and moved behind enemy lines due to using your helmets, I was scared to join missions that involved going into the big mall." Her head slumped out of shame while he stroked her short, soft hair.

Ika, in her curiosity, asked him: "So what the white palace developers put into this helmet that is so powerful and domineering? What does this helmet do to their brains?"

Intelan hesitated for a second, but because of the deep connection he felt to his lover, he replied: "The helmet only makes the user daydream, seeing himself in the virtual world as if he were in reality, but it makes him completely disconnected and blind to the outside world."

She quickly asked him: "You mean the dream actually comes from the user's psyche without your external intervention in the content?"

Intelan thought for a moment and replied: "The contents streamed from the main helmet management server are completely random and are only intended to stimulate the user to dream but not to wake him up, at least that's how I designed the helmet."

Ika pondered: "Is it true that Intelan received an order from the top to give them an opening for penetrating the minds of the helmet users? If so, he would tell me about it, I guess."

The hacking sign was discovered by Intelan on the mall's side, one of the helmets had transmitted hostile codes instead of returning information to the user's thoughts. "Someone tried to infiltrate the packaging company intranet and it comes from the large mall's network. I wonder who's trying to do that. Can you escort me to this point in the mall?" Intelan pointed to a spot that appeared on the hologram screen that was floating in the air.

Ika reacted fearfully to Intelan's words: "Try communicating with them over the network before going out, I'm afraid it's a trap. It is known that the White Palace people always tried to hurt us, the packaging company residents."

Intelan rose angrily and answered Ika: "If so, you are the ones who sent us bullies that hurt innocent consumers. Fortunately, our helmets prevented you from taking over our free market! If you do not intend to help me I will go there myself."

Ika replied: "Would you at least try to communicate with them from a distance, you told me that Georgio hurt you. I'm afraid it's him trying to lure you in." Intelan returned to the console and sent the helmet a signal. Intelan was able to connect to the helmet transmission, presented to them the 3D hologram display of the imagined world by the helmet wearer: a world of nature full of forests all the way across, native-born dwellers in tapered tents in the deep woods. There is a large prairie in the northern area, with a stone fortress around watched by cowboys mounted on horseback, armed with rifles and maintaining a quiet lifestyle. This world was completely different from what Ika and Intelan had ever seen, in terms of display quality everything seemed distant and from an overhead view, they couldn't approach and hear the conversations of the characters moving there. Rayban envisioned this world in a realistic sense, looking at a puddle created in the middle of the forest after the rain, he saw his image reflecting, the body of a brown skin man, wearing animal-skinned clothing and a black braid sliding from his right shoulder. The fresh forest air made him indulge in deep breaths, he heard a scream of a woman calling him back and as he turned he saw a tent and near it, people were sitting around the fire and cooking a freshly hunted animal. Rayban's curiosity made his move toward the horizon outside the woods, where the cowboys rode along with them. He did not expect danger. He was aware that this was a false vision created by the helmet and therefore felt free to take a risk. The cool air chilled his body, making him increase his speed to warm up, operations that were unnecessary in the big, air-conditioned mall always at the perfect temperature. It was precisely the road filled with obstacles from the logs, puddles, and stones that made him feel alive, he was amazed by the sounds of birds making their voices over his head and excited by the sounds of the animals hiding from him behind the bushes. Rayban was actually attached to his helmet, after losing consciousness, his friends connected him to the helmet to try to wake him up from his coma. "The shock he got from the chip made him pass out. Let's hope his brain can operate the helmet." Said his hacker teammate. At the same time at the packaging company, Ika drew Intelan's attention to the scenario that appeared in the helmet display. Rayban was attacked by a horse-drawn cowboy group sitting on a wagon, they fired at him but he continued to run toward the fort surrounded by the wooden fence. As he approached the fort, a figure appeared in the window at the top of the tower, wearing a 19th-century silk dress. He heard a shot that deafened his ears, Rayban turned, and in front of him stood a mounted cowboy wearing the hat, yellow-haired Sonny who looked at him with a mocking smile. Rayban recognized Mazda's figure at the top of the tower and his eyes immediately darkened while he passed out. "We have to follow this broadcast," Ika said. Intelan tried to think about the meaning of the show he had just seen.

Why was the broadcast now stopped? He rewinded the video over and over back to the moment Rayban was hit. "This is the image of the person who envisioned this whole world." Said Intelan enthusiastically, "At the exact moment he was knocked out and fell, the broadcast stopped."

Ika proudly patted Intelan's shoulder: "The hacker tried to penetrate the mall's network through the show or flee to the packaging company, but he was arrested by defense forces."

"Or just simply, he innocently presented what comes up in his subconscious and didn't even try to break in, this helmet has the possibility of a two-sided connection that allows the operator to consciously program it."

Ika said: "This is a hacked helmet? So you say we will have to find out who they are. Let me escort you, my dear, only I can protect you if we will be surprised by the mall state police." Intelan and Ika walked out of the room hand in hand as they headed for the big mall.

Chapter 35

There was no sign of any security breach at the information security wing that Mazda managed. And so she found herself sitting in her office sinking in boredom. When she tried to reflect on her previous life in the packaging company, she couldn't even remember anything, which was very puzzling to her. Mazda suspected that there might be something in the computer systems that kept her from remembering and controlling her thoughts. Mazda tried to find this thing, she hoped to connect with her chip to the White Palace server to recover some of her lost memories. For now, only the desire to meet Sony has to lead her actions. she felt so close to him and still so far from his reach, perhaps it was the feeling that he was sublime and she did not deserve him that kept him away from her for years, even when she was walking around him on the same floor. All that was left for Mazda was to have the courage and to keep track of the White Palace's camera documentation. The cameras monitor the movement of all employees, including Sony. Mazda knew she had the authority and access as the Information Security Chief to look at every employee in the White Palace area and beyond. Mazda moved uncomfortably on the chair in her office, didn't she feel worthy to follow the object of her love? or was it a fear of being caught? "But who's going to catch me?" She thought: "I'm afraid to experience rejection from Sony in a future meeting with him. What if I will be disappointed when I watched him through a camera lens and not in a romantic way like I always imagined?" Her strong urge to work on finding Sonny got over any other life force, whether it be spending time to enjoy herself, eating, or finding a moment of rest under a warm feather bed with another spouse with little kids running around them. Everything stopped until she felt that she was struggling enough to find her loved one that day. Mazda descended on the lower floor of the tower at dusk, afraid of being caught by her superior: the chief of staff, Gogol or Georgio himself, even if she knew that her position as a white palace worker was being monitored with the help of her blood-flowing chip. As she walked towards the cafe where she usually met her shapely friend, she saw swarms of people, the palace workers coming out in a long line from the main gate of the White Palace. Most of them are all crying and whining, some are drooping and mourning, some are upset and talking to their friends in line on the way out. As Mazda sat next to her friend Jivanshi, she noticed a tear on her cheek. Mazda put her hand on her shoulder trying to understand why she was hurting so much, her friend told her: "Most employees, including me, have been fired. Everyone has to leave and become a full-fledged consumer." Mazda was shocked and realized that even her days were numbered, even though she had not received a message instructing her to leave the palace.

"Don't worry, you won't be fired. They are only removing the creative, opinionated, and aesthetic creators. For some reason, they have no use for us at the White Palace." She said to Mazda, who listened in silence.

Jivanshi continued: "My husband, the gardener, is also deported. It turns out that nanobots can design a wonderful garden without the delicacy and soul that beats in the big heart of this wonderful man I found. Maybe you could escort us to the Big Mall? Show us a place where we can find some sleeping capsules in a nice area." Mazda did not hesitate and immediately got out of her chair about a second after Jivanshi, they joined in line with her husband and two children. The innocent children did not know what was going on because they were given the imaging helmet so as not to witness the harsh spectacle of a convoy of people weeping for their fate.

Mazda asked Jivanshi: "What are you so worried about? You won't have to work one more day in your life, you will be free like the rest of the mall's consumers." Mazda who understood the trauma of leaving the palace and comfort life tried to cheer up her good friend, but she immediately replied: "This plot to give us up as employees is very cruel to my liking, for me not to create and design is a kind of detachment from my very existence when I do not create all day it's immediately overwhelmed me like A black hole of emptiness as if my body is filled with a poisonous air that makes me dizzy and presses me hard on my heart until it explodes. "

On their way to the train station leading to a more remote part of the mall, Mazda encountered a middle-aged woman shouting at her. At first Jivanshi, her husband, and Mazda did not realize she was screaming in their direction but then they turned around and heard what she had to say: "You sold my daughter a helmet since then she does not talk to me, just sitting in a chair, sometimes walking while daydreaming when the helmet hides her face down to her mouth. She neither communicates with me nor with her surroundings, she refuses to remove the helmet. What is this disease that you brought to her? "

Mazda answered her: "How do you know I sold her the helmet?" At that moment, she felt as if an arrow had struck her heart when she realized that she had hurt someone dear to someone.

The woman approached them and said to her: "You sold the helmet to me. I thought I would give her a nice gift for a discounted price. It was one day's rent I could afford to give up. The real cost is to lose my daughter." Mazda intended to explain to her that she didn't really know what the helmet could do, but the woman had already moved away.

Most of the residents of the mall were mesmerized by the helmet, walking around or sitting unaware of the physical reality around them, most of them looked too exhausted to walk and some of them seemed shriveled as no food pill had been inserted into their bodies for a long time. Wonder how they move and live as if they are not flesh and blood. Jivanshi looked anxiously at her children who were confused and quiet and unaware of her sadness. When they arrived at the door of a capsule shop that boasted a flashing "Dream Hotel" sign, Mazda turned to the couple with a smile that found it hard to hide the embarrassment and sorrow: "I wish you a good, peaceful life, here you will not have to worry about your children's well being, they will continue to be happy." And finally, Mazda quoted a sentence that Georgio conceived and was told in front of hundreds of thousands of broadcasters on the state intranet: "You are the consumers who control the mall and steer it from one success to another." Mazda turned her head in humiliation following what she said and walked back towards the train cart which would take her back to the White Palace. At the same time, Jivanshi and her husband each removed the addictive helmet from their children to try to put them to sleep in the sleeping capsule. As soon as the capsule closed, she started singing a soothing lullaby until they fell asleep while the little one sucked his finger. Jivanshi kissed her husband and went into a separate capsule away from her husband who had to give up his wife's warm body tonight. With her eyes closed to the capsule entertainment interface, Jivanshi chose to scribble in virtual brushes all kinds of designs, shapes, and characters. She felt genuine release and comfort from her sadness as she worked.

Chapter 36

Georgio opened the consultants' meeting discussing the organizational changes that occurred in the White Palace. Gogol read the agenda: "It seems that thanks to the automation of imagination and creativity through the helmets, we are at the beginning of a new era of increasing the company's profitability." Gogol was amazed by his words, if the human imagination was really mechanized successfully, it was a historical achievement that could lead to an unknown place. After Georgio's words, there was an awkward silence from the counselors who felt the sword of dismissal on their necks.

Georgio asked Gogol: "And what about the political situation in the mall?"

Gogol replied: "The rents will be waived until the election of the Prime Minister of the mall State will be over, we must decide which candidate we support.

Georgio snapped at Gogol's words: "After Peugeot will resign, we will support the candidate I recommended."

The Political Affairs Advisor suddenly stood up, gaining courage and responding to Georgio's words: "It's important not to look like we have recommended. Consumers must understand that you control them ruthlessly and some are frustrated by the power of the helmets, so we should not openly recommend a particular candidate." Georgio waved his hand dismissively at the counselor who immediately sat down. Gogol as he went on to say: "What is certain is that we must control this candidate, it will never occur to him that he is acting on his own, and most importantly, that no other candidate will suddenly emerge." Georgio laughed, with all the consultants around him, he always felt he is in a warm family atmosphere but one where he felt the most important and powerful of all, like an iron cradle swinging and being its lead. Such a family atmosphere has never been part of his life. Whenever he felt that depression and loneliness prevailed, Georgio called for a conference session to uplift his soul. After most of the White Palace workers were laid off, he felt his strong grip is loosening.

"And what about the technical side of operating such a large amount of helmets?" Georgio said as he leaned back on his adjustable chair.

One of the advisers who feared being punished for not participating stood up and exclaimed loudly: "As it seems at this time, the master server is working at 70% of its capability, which means that the helmet management capability is working properly, the data flow is being

204

analyzed quickly enough, and the processor is analyzing the data, distributes them back to the chip subjects properly and randomly according to statistical analysis... "

Georgio interrupted him and said: "And how do you think this dissipation is done? Do you trust this algorithm programmed by Intelan that no longer works here?"

The consultant standing and no one saw his trembling feet answered a few seconds later: "As one who has worked with Intelan and has known him for many years, I can assure you that he has developed a high-quality code to take care of..." The consultant paused at the sight of Georgio's raised hand in front of everyone calling the end of the session.

After the meeting had dissipated, Georgio took the helmet sample that had been thrown on the conference table and attached it to his forehead as both of his eyes were closed. Watching his eyes he saw himself standing beside his late father, it felt more real to him than a memory or a daydream. The cool air of the mall blend was shone in front of him, the lights dazzled him and the crowd standing around the stage where he and his father stood was noisy and looked very much alive in the most realistic way he had ever experienced. Looking at his body, he felt himself as thin as a teenager, if he had a mirror he would immediately look at his reflection, but he couldn't help but look at his father's face who ignored him and spoke intently to the huge crowd of the big mall. Except for his father's existence and the young structure of his body, nothing had changed in the big mall, the concentration of stores connected to each other in shimmering ivory that connected to the great dome that encompassed everything that was known to the world several hundred feet above the mall floor. After Georgio's admiration, he was able to listen to his father's speech: "For several generations, I and my ancestors have kept you safe from the radiation, cold, heat, and terrors of nature. We have raised many families here who enjoy freedom from bondage, I would not want you to suffer as my ancestors and other families who lived without the protection of the big mall. Your consumerism guarantees the survival of the economic cycle that maintains the strength of the mall state. " The audience became enthusiastic and following the rhetorical speech Georgio's father came to the point: "I convened you here because I am uncomfortable with this stagnation, and so I want to tell you the truth. After the collapse of the old world due to natural disasters that caused economic collapse and a greater natural disaster, the rest of humankind, your ancestors, were gathered into a huge building that served as an old state experimental building. What I want to tell you is that if you thought the big mall enveloped the entire existing world it was a deception, the mall was just a tiny part of what is called Earth. " At that moment there was an explosion that hit the father of young Georgio. He foresaw his fall to the ground just as he was finishing the sentence, the upset crowd didn't understand the meaning of the speech and engaged in a hysterical scramble following the fall of the father while repressing the last sentences spoken. Georgio was completely obliterated by his father's words, he did not believe he could reveal this secret, but was angry with those who hurt him only because he wanted to reveal it. When Georgio removed the helmet and returned thirty years back from his memoir to the conference room, he thought of one thing: to Punish the packaging company that caused his father's death. "It was only in her interest to prevent the spread of the gospel of the true size of the big mall," he thought at that moment. The dependence of the Great Mall on the supply of raw materials from the outside world made her do the nefarious act of silencing his father so violently. Georgio was never told the reason or moment when his father was killed, at the very moment of the assassination, he was in a private room at the palace. His late mother was beside his father at that moment and what he experienced in the helmet's vision was only a slight distortion of the past sent to him without his request. But where did the message was sent to his helmet from??

Chapter 37

Rayban's gang had a small number of medical nanobots stolen from the academy lab that they hacked for medical purposes. These nanobots smacked into Rayban's chest, the second strike made Rayban's head shine, which lit up like a night lamp in the dark, hidden room. The group waited a few minutes for the moment he wake up from his coma and to their delight, this moment came when he raise his head feeling sleepy. One of his friends, Lenov, the brown-skinned and rounded mane of hair, was the first to look at Rayban when his eyes first opened: "I managed to translate the signals in your brain into a clear video, come and see where you were, Rayban, my dear brother," but the object of his requests was barely recovered from the dream.

Rayban muttered as he tried to focus, "I saw Sony, he was holding a bottle like on an advertisement."

His second short and skinny friend, Nikeo, grabbed Rayban's left palm and asked, "Why would you dream of Sony? Could he have also made you fall in love with him like half the mall's women?" He smirked mockingly.

Rayban was able to sit down, took a deep breath, and said while coughing between each sentence: "It may not have been a dream. I have never watched his commercials or purchased this drink. I suppose this information has taken over my daydreaming process. It entered inside my helmet. even now, I can't stop thinking about this drink. Longing for it... the passion. "

Rayban fainted but Nikeo shook his face while his eyes closed: "Tell us about the content of the dream, where have you been? What have you done there?" Lenov asked Nikeo: "The covert broadcasts that been sent by anyone who wants to influence consumers at the mall coming from the chip to the helmet should be considered." Rayban awoke again as he breathed and exhaled, despite experiencing many chases and encounters with the mall's state security forces, he never experienced a trauma that was actually caused by a virtual encounter.

"I want to meet her again, where is she?"

"who are you talking about?" asked him Lenov.

Nikeo spoke into Rayban's eyes: "Forget about her, she's a spy who is playing with you, I recognize her as such. You need to be one to recognize one."Rayban abandoned them and began to walk toward the exit of the group's hiding place. Lenov stopped Nikeo who was about to jump on Rayban who walked in a slow-motion as he appeared to be sleepwalking, signaling that he'd better accompany him. But Rayban was not sleepwalking, he was awake and passionate because of the addiction and brainwashing he went through, the thirst for a bottle of a drink was completely real. He saw in his mind the drops that were sipped by Sony, also sipped by him. He was intrigued to know what was in the drink, and what it tasted even if he knew that this liquid was nothing more than a hologram that would not be projected beyond his jaw. The sensation in his lips felt completely real, he was curious about the taste that is essentially just an electrical current in his nerves. When Rayban arrived and sat at the hologram liquor bar, he was approached by a knotted and ripped bartender with a virtual hairstyle and virtual colored uniform and before he opened his mouth to the question Rayban answered while sitting relaxed and smiling: "The golden drink". For only five Eullars he sipped a drink, and another and another, with no effect on his stimulus threshold or stomach, but with a real impact on his bill that was starting to grow. When his account reached zero, Rayban sank into deep depression and emptiness, later his two friends joined him and waited patiently for him to finish drinking. During this time, they reflected on the significance of what was happening to Rayban, which has happened to many consumers. Lenov and Nikeo swept the exhausted Rayban as he dragged his feet on the gleaming marble floor of the Big mall. Lenov recalls how the three teenage friends started stealing food pellets from Georgio's restaurants, it was a juvenile hobby. Rayban was the initiator, Lenov was the hacker to the restaurant computer and the thin little Nikeo sneaked and stole the pills. This operation was of no importance or gain to them, no one needed more than nine pills a day, rich in vitamins and minerals for three meals a day. In any case, they collected the pills and hid them in empty stores without any use, they used to sleep in the stores that were looted by them instead of sleeping like their family members in their capsules. In the abandoned store, they had a great mall's intranet and lots of privacy that allowed them to play games like regular kids. To this day, they are forced to flee from one empty store to another each time the first store goes back to be operational. Occasionally they managed to get a job at the White Palace store, but when they got into trouble they had to run away. When they returned to the empty store with the energetically squeezed Rayban, the three lay on the floor of the store as their two other friends watch the store entrance. Suddenly the front door gleamed, a sign that someone outside wanted to enter the store. The rest of the group stood on maximum alert, even Rayban managed to pull himself up and hold onto the end of the desk on which the main terminal computer stood.

"We received no indication that the mall police is on her way here, Are there any curious people at the door? Should we ignore it or run away?" Nikeo said in a panicked voice. Lenov raised his hand to Nikeo to signal him to calm down and relax. One of their gatekeepers peeked and signaled that there were two people, a man and a woman waiting outside the door.

Ika told Intelan: "According to the reception of my radar, there is no one in this room. It may have been abandoned and it was the center of an intrusive networking activity in the past." Intelan thought Ika was wrong. In fact, beyond the door, the band could disrupt radio frequencies engulfed in the walls of the room and a message was sent that it was empty. And so it happened that Intelan's great curiosity overcame the fear and they both burst through the door. Intelan was taken aback by the people in front of him, Ika jumped with a belligerent leap in front of him with her arms like two menacing spears. At that moment the two gatekeepers flinched back and Lenov pulled Rayban and fled back.

Nikeo with his sharp, quick senses realized that he was not in danger and shouted: "They are not cops, wait a minute, relax!"

Intelan shouted, "I'm not a cop, I'm from the White Palace." The shocked Ika turned her head to him and was amazed by his revealing answer. As soon as she turned her head to Intelan one of the group members attacked her but she kicked him with a crushing blow on the floor.

Intelan called out to the horrified crowd: "We didn't come here to hurt you, just to see how you guys work on the intranet, I developed this system but I have long since abandoned the White Palace. I was afraid that you were the messengers who hacked into the packaging company. What do you plan to do to the mall state's system? "

Lenov operated a system that surrounded Ika and Intelan with holograms of beautiful dresses previously sold at the abandoned store. The dresses swirled in the air around the couple in an electric tornado-like that locked them up. Ika was neutralized and fainted, only Intelan remained standing while the vortex subsided until it disappeared. "We don't trust you and your friend, it seems that by her gray and tangible attire she is the packaging company citizen. You claim you came from the White Palace we are trying to overthrow. Why should we rely on you not to betray us, did you come from the White Palace to serve as a double agent?"Rayban said firmly to Intelan. Intelan hesitated and replied: "Don't hurt me, I promise not to reveal your location to the Grand Georgio, the truth is that I'm afraid to go back to work for him after he hurt me. I'll do everything to prove my loyalty to you." Intelan cried.

"If you want to prove your loyalty, you need to help Rayban to wean off from the helmet. Do you have any idea how to break into it?" Intelan approached Rayban and put his helmet on his head, after a brief analysis of the pattern projected into his brain he managed to undo the effect of the ad he was addicted to. "Let him and Ika sleep. They both need a rest, we'll talk later." Said Intelan and lay down on the floor of the store.

Chapter 38

The prime-time news broadcast opened with the announcement of a promising new candidate for the premiership elections. The news anchor described candidate Renault: "He has worked his way as the Southern Division's consumer leader for years, growing up in a family with many children, and over the years has emerged as a savvy consumer who wasted over 50,000eulars in one day who he managed to save by partnering with other friends," the presenter continued In a description that reads: "He stood out as a leader who united the "savvy consumer movement" that opposed the exclusive control of the Democratic Alliance of the big mall Ltd., now making a move against the leading candidate Peugeot who resigned as former prime minister and is running a re-election campaign." Sunan and Fox waited for the lead anchor to call them to report the story they have Filmed at the packaging company, Sunan seemed particularly tense even though her story was complete, and she was able to note all the sculptures on display and all the events that happened during Subaru's conduct, including the interview with her, but for some reason, she felt there is a sting missing in her article, though she also managed to sum up what had happened in the packaging company, Sunan felt certain words were sitting on the edge of her tongue and had trouble remembering them. If her brain cells could sweat they would draw their liquids out of her eyes to gather the information together for some conclusion or memory she had in her brain when she was outside the mall. Fox took the opportunity to pull her arm while saying, "Darling, we are called to the studio." Sunan and Fox sat down, and within a few moments the show's host turned to the viewers and proclaimed the headline: "Fox and Sunan's story." These words made Sunan nervous with a fake smile as she had been used to for years. The one who had started to open his mouth was Fox: "For the sake of the viewers, we went into the packaging company's premises, the body that is supposed to provide the big mall with the most important raw materials for its existence..." After a few minutes of a graphic description narrated by Fox, Sunan continued: "Examine the new exhibit that has invested a lot of resources from the packaging company repository, resources that are highly doubtful whether they will be beneficial to either the packaging company or the big mall, and I will elaborate. " Sunan described in detail the flipped car model in which its strange and complex structure would draw visitors to the packaging company. In addition, Sunan described the music hall that played classical music from the beginning of the industrial era to electronic music from the end of the first consumer era. Sunan has featured numerous pictures and verbal descriptions of the great and historical exhibition that could cause, in her words, " visitors and casual tourists to be incited by nostalgia to the old world as well as loyal consumers and rebels." At the end of the article, the anchor smiled at her, and Sunan and Fox walked out of the studio. Fox smiled with a satisfied-looking face and Sunan with a worried and bitter one.

The chief lobbyist news editor stopped Sunan in the hallway, calling her for an eye-to-eye meeting in her office located on a very high floor in the White Palace tower. The priestess started by saying, "I want you to interview OUR candidate." Sunan was surprised by the special request, so far she has not been asked to rub shoulders with important high-ranking people.

The priestess continued: "As the chief hostess, I have to make the public not resent the Great Holy One, the living God, Georgio, and so we have appointed a candidate for our sake to sweep away the disgruntled masses left to vote. And, of course, after his election, he will remain loyal to us."

Sunan was intrigued and asked: "You must be talking about Peugeot being forced to resign, he was our candidate? Why do you think he can continue?" The lobbyist smirked, signaling Sunan with her hand to stop talking.

She stood up and looked out the window outside the White Palace wall: "You probably see that all the loyalists for the big mall Consumerism also use the vast majority of helmets and pose no threat. In fact, we can make them not vote at all, which will help us direct the vote to a candidate everybody would be happy to vote to, even the helmet users. Sunan began to understand the agenda of the articles she was asked to write and decided to show her support by saying: "You mean I will help you convince the disgruntled White Palace public in my articles that the non-Peugeot candidate will support their interest and thus you will prevent another candidate out of your control to win the elections."

 The priestess laughed out loud: "Is it true that my work is very creative and fun? Would you believe that I conceived the idea, I passed it on to Georgio's advisor and he approved the action! You must have heard of our candidate Renault, I ask you to present him as the most outrageous candidate that ever endangered the perfection of the big mall. " Sunan was shocked, the two seconds of her stuttering lasted forever, in this eternity there was a war going on in her delicate soul. She did not imagine that the most important interview of her life would actually be a sophisticated chess exercise designed to fool the masses. Leaving the room after agreeing to the interview, she contacted Fox to meet him at the entrance of the capsule where Renault used to sleep: "We will surprise him in a festive interview tomorrow morning. This rebel leader will not know where it came from." Fox was thrilled with the mission like a child, not knowing that Sunan keeps the secret in her heart, and felt deep shame.

Chapter 39

The two final candidates reached the home stretch of the election campaign, Renault and Peugeot who have so far announced their candidacy for the premier of the mall state were on their way to present their agenda at the newsroom studio in the White Palace. At the center of the studio were the show host and the two candidates on both sides. To the right, Peugeot sat relaxed but his face seemed impassive and lifeless as if he had been forced to reach the distinguished moment on this festive day. On the other side, Renault, the new candidate to replace Peugeot, was smiling and looking fresh and energized. Renault waited for a moment to be allowed to lead the big mall, even if it was apparently. He had this sentence memorized in his mind: "To omit the word: apparently," he was prepared to storm Peugeot with allegations: the allegedly failed prime minister. The program aired from an open studio in the White Palace's main entertainment area, a crowd of mall workers, the few remaining, gathered to cheer or to revile the candidates as if it were a battle of gladiators from ancient Rome. The host began the confrontation with a description of the candidates and a polite address to both of them.

Then he began to ask the difficult questions, Peugeot was asked by the host: "Mr. Prime Minister How do you intend to explain the failure to stop the packaging company troops invasion? Why were the police not prepared to repel this attack?"

Renault erupted as he shouted, interrupting Peugeot from answering: "Because of such a failure you are not fit to be elected, no one cares what excuse you are going to make!"

Peugeot broadcast a private message to Renault's chip: "Why are you excited, do you really think I will answer this question seriously?"

Renault calmed down and Peugeot replied: "Due to low taxation, I had to cut the police protection budget in favor of a suitable universal minimum wage for the residents of the mall, as well as the maintenance of the White Palace priests' maintenance services..."

This time the host interrupted him: "Why have you not strengthened the priesthood services in previous years? It is known that mall workers and priests who supervise them are a spiritual foundation that protects the mall!" The host read the text from a teleprompter hologram floating in front of him.

Peugeot answered tiredly to the perplexing question: "Because this year, I wanted to increase the White Palace's priesthood budget and, on the other hand, reduce the corporate tax collected from mall stores, thereby increasing the universal salary of 100 Eular per consumer. This is why I had no choice but to cut the police budget.

The host addressed Renault: "Have you seen the difficult dilemmas Peugeot has to deal with, how do you with the experience of a leader and a consumer intend to lead an entire mall?"

Renault replied at ease: "There is a whole public of white palace workers and shops who are struggling to provide the mall's consumers with excellent service. I have never seen how they live. Some say they get huge rooms for accommodation. I would like this information to be transparent to everyone."

Gogol just burst in anger into Renault's chip and yelled at him: "Don't forget I listen to you and guide you how to talk. We agreed that you don't reveal secrets from the White Palace if you want to win."

Renault sent Gogol an inter-chip text message while speaking in front of the camera at the studio: "You must let me speak in a way that will surprise those who listen to me. In the end, I'm not really going to reveal what's happening between the

White Palace walls, let me spice up the conversation so I will be noticed. "

Gogol snapped at Renault: "Don't disclose any information that viewers are unaware of, conduct the debate at a superficial level, do you understand?" Gogol disconnected from the call and at the same time turned off the hologram broadcast at his room. His penetration into Renault's chip reminded him of his particular problem: the loss of memory caused by the main server with the help of the chip in his body, as Professor Quelcomizki with whom he had consulted recently, had verified that fact.

At the end of the broadcast Renault was asked to go to Gogol's room. Renault left the newsroom in the White Palace square. For the first time in his life, the blue-gray hologram suit he wore slightly concealed the tremor in his body. Not only did Renault marvel at the huge structure that surrounded him as he walked the central square of the White Palace, but also the verve and activation of passersby who seemed independent and satisfied. All the stories he heard about the life of slavery in the White Palace were shattered in an instant against the sights that appeared before his eyes. Renault went to the elevator in the big tower that led him to Gogol's room. Gogol greeted him with a polite, tiny smile with his shoulders lowered. Renault sat on a softer couch than any chair he ever sat on,

Gogol looked at him with a piercing look: "Now you see the truth, we are not slaves. Georgio takes care of his employees and gives them the best conditions, yet he invests many resources to hide it."

Renault interrupted Gogol's words, "What will you do to me, erase my memory? You can't threaten me anymore!" Gogol yelled at him to shut up. He took a holographic glass of water, sipped from it, and said calmly: "Do you see this glass? It is not made of solid material but can contain water in it. You too, like this hologram glass, can seem to contain anything, if we want to increase your power. But if you don't, your content will spill over to the floor. " Renault rose to his feet and said, "Enough, I will not tolerate these threats. I will be the Prime Minister who will not listen to you!" Renault burst through the door that opened and immediately closed before he could pass until it nearly hit his nose. He turned to Gogol who turned over to Renault: "Last sentence, we will give you the stick or the carrot after you finish your tenure as prime minister. You and your children will have a decent job and residence for generations, or you prefer to fight us... that would be a shame." After Renault thoughtfully left the room, Gogol sent a message to Georgio that he was interested in a face-to-face meeting on a personal issue. The request was approved.

Chapter 40

In the packaging company where transcription level genetically modified humans are becoming hybrids, Subara was the only one left with a pure human genetic expression since birth. After a long time when Subara refused to be fed with the nano-capsule engineered food containing RANs that was changing her Species and type, she increasingly felt her humanity in the solitary sense of the word. After all that time she managed to juggle between all the technical consultants, tough executives, hardworking and brutal soldiers, she noticed that her social skills surpassed anyone around her including her beloved Cisco. Cisco has long been looking for a different interest with its new half-breed human friends, the Pitbulls, Activities like assault games, running sprints, and mischief in small groups have brought him great pleasure. Cisco preferred to give up Subara's overly sophisticated human warmth, full of intrigue and gossipy thoughts in addition to her takeover of him. Thus they found themselves very far out of the ordinary working hours. Subaru's loneliness was very burdensome to her, once she was the "queen of bees" who felt a deep purpose sown to the bones, and now felt incapable of finding anyone to interact with as she lusted. Subara tried to come up with a way to stop the genetic feeding of company employees," so dedicated and loyal to the company that they forgot to take care of themselves and communicate like humans", Subara thought to herself. The loneliness and growing lack of communication with Cisco allowed her to express the meaning of her total humanity in her words. Subara intrigued to see people like her: non-engineered, went to the packaging company's exhibition avenues. There she thought about meeting and trying to talk to immigrants from the Big mall for pleasure or at least for research purposes. The temporary immigrants who dined from the engineered food during their stay at the packaging company after a few days took the form of one of the imprisoned animals and pushed themselves to work in the company's service. Subara enjoyed the frequent tours each morning at the New World Music Hall of Fame which was converted from an old concrete factory. As she listened to compositions of the classical period that orchestras from the distant past played or the sounds of guitar and noisy electronics, she talked to immigrants about cultural experiences. She realized how genetic capsules saturated diet led most of them to gradually become more bees with a hairier face and buzzing sound, they lost their patience staying at the exhibition and felt a strong need for productive work. For weeks, Subara toured the new museums she created and saw how human migrants who were exemplary conversationalists, became frantic and intelligent pitbull hybrids with limited human communication skills. After a week of touring around the company in a false identity, Subara woke up in her bed with a smile as Cisco was awake beside her as he needed only a few hours of sleep, though she felt less lonely and sad. It was the day when the company's general board meeting was held, on such a day she conducted an orchestra of executives and felt like a real queen with all the spotlight pointing at her. Subara felt that she could easily get into the pink-oval dress that had been hanging in the closet for decades from her previous queen's term. While looking in the mirror and discovering that the dress's bee-like structure did not allow her to fit in comfortably and tightly, Cisco politely called her outside the door. She opened the electric door for him and he emerged through the hallway. He admired her beauty and even took out his tongue, she made sure to close his muzzle from drooling. Without further ado, he grabbed her hand and wrapped his arm around her as they walked out together as a couple to the general conference hall. She looked at Cisco and felt she still loved him the way he was, but she felt a little twinge in her heart because of the fact she could never love anyone more than she love him. The board meeting opened, everyone sat in a circle, each sat on a standard chair except for Subara's chair, to her left sat the head of the owls. The pupils of his eyes were enlarged and he exhaled heavily, there was no trace of any feathers, since he was originally a human being. To her right sat the head of the Agama, they looked almost like human beings only with certain distortions of the skin that were greener and stiffer and their tongues occasionally protruding outward. They suffered slight deformity of the limbs, their elbows regularly inclined upwards. To the right of the ant committee, the head of the Pitbull Workers' Guard sat who had not long ago attacked the mall state. Until recently, he was the head of the watchdog staff, which was upgraded to a more aggressive Pitbulls. Next to them, Cisco sat, and to his right the head of the bee-people that was a distant relative of Queen Subara. There didn't seem to be any warm and cordial connection between them. The tension of the committee's members was extremely heavy, they wanted to raise the issue of immigrants.

The person who initiated and endorsed it was the head of the Owl Committee who stood up and said, "Your Highness, I will let you open the meeting." Subara nodded, feeling that she knew what the rep was going to talk about, but she gave him the right of way: "As you know, the packaging company is a masterpiece for work and research, recently opened its doors to visitors, some call them immigrants."

Cisco stood up in defense of his queen and stopped the owl's representative speech: "You mean the wise decision of the bee queen, anyone who has a problem with this decision shall rise immediately!" The heads of the committees felt uncomfortable and whispered to each other until the representative continued: "We couldn't help but notice the full integration of all visitors as full-time employees into the company's departments after a few days off."

Subara replied: "So what is the problem? That was my goal in the first place, to strengthen the packaging company versus the big mall." Subara was silent as she looked into the owl-man's enlarged eyes.

"I do not claim that your actions did not result from good intentions, but you cannot fail to see that those immigrants were not properly educated, and loading them with a genetic baggage does not change the fact that they are not culturally educated after living their entire lives as consumer humans." The other leaders joined the owl man's words and spoke loudly until silenced by Cisco getting upset and standing up from his chair.

Subara calmed him down and he sat down: "So do you claim that there is no improvement in the immigrants' production compared to the natives despite the same genetic charge that should fit them into their duties?"

The owl replied without flinching: "Yes, my queen, the lack of proper education seems to cause much friction in the owl's research institutes, the military discipline of the vigilantes, and the ragged work ethic of the bee people out of the immigrant population."

The head of the bee workers' committee rose to her feet and said in a squeaky voice: "They are lazy and not conducive to work, they should be expelled!" Immediately there were shouts of anyone present in the room for only a few seconds until Subara silenced them with the wave of her hand. Subara got up from her chair and was about to leave the conference room, she said her last words: "I decided as the undisputed leader of the packaging company and as the bee queen to change the feeding system in the company. From now on, no more genetic repair material will be absorbed in the food. Immigrants will be assimilated into the population and will not harm the production of the company. " Subara threw a bomb into the room and left calmly. She envisioned how the change would benefit her packaging company friends, and the ease she would have in living with ordinary people like her.

Chapter 41

Mazda continued her tedious search for Sony. Every day she sat for hours facing raw data or security footage of passers-by in the White Palace but failed to find him. No chip has been created on Sony's identity: "Is it possible that there is no chip in his body? How can I extract information about a person's identity and name according to the chip in his body?" Nor was she able to completely decipher the data obtained in the security interface. One of the functions of the system was the selection of prohibited words in human thought that was scanned by the chip. Mazda concluded that the only way to know about Sony was to find the location where the commercials are filmed in the White Palace. She found an excuse to search the marketing department under the pretext of an investigation to meet him, she planed it so that it looked completely professional. One morning, Mazda convened five of her subordinate executives: "After a comprehensive scan of the marketing department's chips, I had a reasonable suspicion of collusion. It turns out that the hackers and the graphic content of the commercials are people from the marketing system itself." Mazda's employees were shocked: "We thought these were rebels hiding in the mall's big store. You told us yourself you were locating their whereabouts and intending to try to catch them red-handed," said one of the managers in amazement.

Mazda replied to her in an answer she had prepared in advance: "Then it turns out that I was misled and the sabotage was caused by the marketing department." Another security manager told Mazda with a derisive tone: "From what I understand, you have been nominated because you know the insurgent character from the outside, how would you treat the enemies on the inside if you do not know the white palace inside and out?" Her subordinate managers did not like the quick promotion she received for her inexperience, now she commands them. So she made it difficult to answer questions, Mazda shouted at everyone: "No one is going to drive me crazy with unnecessary questions, you have received your instructions, now I must understand completely and definitively that this is not the White Palace marketing department. Tomorrow I want to go in there to do a full physical scan of the chips without any exceptions". One of the managers burst out assertively: "You intend to scan the information systems as well, not just the working persons, right?" Mazda ignored her and walked out of the room, after she left the room she was feeling scared until tears came down her face, she had never been so close to Sony and so far away.

The next morning Mazda and the five security managers entered the main photographic studio in the marketing wing, which was located on the middle floor of the tower. A solemn adult, dressed in hologram robes, approached Mazda: "What makes you think you have a right to get into the sanctum of commercials?" The rest of the security managers bowed to him with their faces facing the floor. Only Mazda stood in front of him and stammered in that position, she noticed that she was the only one wearing a formal work suit while the executives wore a white robe and were barefoot in honor of one of the most sacred places in the commercial company where the spiritual work of marketing White Palace's products is made. Without any awareness of the severity of the capacity in terms of the other people in the room, Mazda blurted out: "I really didn't come here to interrupt, but as the Information Security Chief, I am committed to checking every person in the studio including the actors, if their chip is valid and transmits without any kind of hacks."

The producing priest continued to stand at the entrance to the hall leading to the other rooms on the main floor and main studio: "You have to explain to me why you can't scan the chips from your office, surely you have the means to do that, do you have a convincing explanation?" He answered angrily as the light air conditioner waved his gray, lonely strand of hair on his forehead.

Mazda answered him impatiently: "If you must know, there are serious suspicions that one of your employees is helping some terrorists to damage the advertising set and is the one who initiates the injury ..."

The priest was stunned by Mazda's reluctance at the sacredness of the place and her insensitivity to trampling so firmly on the most important place in the big mall. "I authorize you to come in and do a quick check, to remove any suspicion from this place, but don't think I won't report to His Holiness Georgio for the blasphemy that you have done here." The priest finished his speech and moved to the side of the wall. He was clinging to the wall for Mazda to move on with the five escorts who had just gotten up after bowing. They each split into a different room in the marketing department, Mazda rushed to the main studio where a new commercial starring her loved one has been filmed for many years, the yellow-haired Sony. Mazda passed through the studio doors that opened automatically in her face when she saw the set with the actors and a floating camera aimed at them. Mazda's gaze stared at bare-breasted Sony, only a Roman-style tunic on half of his chest, all dressed in bronze tone and his short hair flapping with the artificial wind as he smiled at the camera. Her eyesight blurred while she was out of breath, she found it difficult to stand on her feet, as their gazes intersected, saying, "I've come to do a review..." and then fainted. She woke up after being given an adrenaline rush by a small medical robot aiming an infrared bulb directly into her eyes to perform a system scan. Mazda's adrenaline in her body rise and got her buttocks up until she stood on her feet, realizing that Sony had already disappeared from the film set. She pushed the robot sideways to the amazement of the cast, the film crew, and the rest of the production staff because within seconds she had passed from sleep mode to run mode towards the locker rooms. She came to the room with a huge sign written "Sony" on it and another "Forbidden Entry" sign. When she came in, she saw a naked, tall, pale, and stoop-shouldered man looking with a sad face at the mirror, with nobody's tone, his hair a little balding, and his makeup-free face peeking out the wrinkles of a middle-aged man.

The clumsy man hid his underwear in Tunic and said to her in a calm voice, "Why did you come in without tapping the door?"

The stunned Mazda stammered: "Are you ... are you Sony?"

Sony answered, "Why do you look surprised? As you know, I've been leading the campaigns of the big mall for decades. Did you really think my projected image was the same as my image in reality?"

Mazda stammered: "I imagined you different, you are my favorite, what did they do to a star like you?"

Sony replied: "I'm not really loved, I'm not a star, just a slave who has long since disappeared. I have been used as a symbol and kept alive for many years. Please, if you can help me escape here, I will give up my external image, just To go free. "

Mazda replied weakly: "I can't do anything, I just wanted to see you." Mazda was about to leave the room, her heart trembling and her face was even paler than Sonny's face. "Goodbye ma'am, I was glad to meet you." Those were the last words he said before she slammed the door.

Chapter 42

Georgio sat next to his son's crib, the baby slept soundly. He noticed how his baby exhaled air that puff the curl over his forehead. Georgio mused to himself, as bitterness wrapped his heart: "I have to dismantle the packaging company no matter what, I have to remove it from my private compound." Georgio's secretary walked into his room which had the highest view of the big mall and told him that Gogol was waiting for him outside. Georgio ordered the secretary to bring him in.

Gogol's look was desperate, Georgio smiled slightly when he saw him: "What's so important to you have to let me know? Don't you see I'm busy in the high room?" Said Georgio as he stared at Gogol, who was with his head lowered.

Gogol felt he had to say what is in its heart: "Great Georgio, you know I admire you and trust you with my eyes closed, but I have to understand why I don't remember my past, the childhood from which I started this life."

Georgio was surprised and stood up and went over to Gogol: "You think I didn't follow you when you were investigating in the archives and the academy? I knew you were looking for something on a personal level, but, interestingly, it's about your private memory."

Gogol looked into Georgio's old eyes: "I found out you were corrupting my memory with the chip in my body."

Georgio chuckled and answered his advisor: "I have no fear of you, why should I hide information from you? How about I give you a chance to take a look at your past without the chip?"

Gogol who was naturally suspicious asked: "How are you going to remove the chip from my body?"

Georgio looked out the window as a train pulled away into the horizon towards the south. Georgio signaled his finger over there: "Go to the Southern Packaging Company, they will remove the chip for you as they do to anyone who goes to their border. If you happen to remember something beyond what you knew, I won't stop it."

"What are you asking for in return?"

Gogol asked, "I want you to embark on a peace deal with the packaging company. The packaging company has decided to lure our consumers into a real-world viewing experience of objects from the outside world, causing us a loss of helmet users."

Gogol had to ask, "And you want to make peace in exchange for agreeing to stop luring civilians into their field?"

Georgio replied to Gogol as he turned to him: "The Peace Initiative is just an excuse to get you into the packaging company as a Trojan horse. You have to sabotage their food production system and implant medical nanobots that disrupt the food's genetic composition and poison it imperceptibly and slowly."

"The insertion of a deadly virus into the cells of the body"? Gogol was startled for a moment: "There will be a brutal war if they will ever find out I had anything to do with it. Why take so many human lives just to keep our consumers out of the packaging company?"

Georgio commanded him: "No questions! Get out or send someone else on to the mission!" Gogol was about to head to the lower-floor chip-making factory to get some nanobots done, not before Georgio told him, "Just know that you probably won't remember anything, because I didn't hide anything from you."

Gogol listened to Georgio and finally answered, "Your Holiness, why do you trust me?"

Georgio immediately replied: "You have a great talent and you have made a career on your own. Your recipe for success is simple: in your head, you stick to the goal and in your heart, you do what is right for you." In your case, you are good at mesmerizing and convincing people. "
Traveling to the southern part of the big mall takes a few hours by train from the White Palace, a speed where you can't see the view, just the mall's glass ceiling. Gogol sat in the magnificent cart, isolated from the other passengers protected by two guards. The last time he met Subara for diplomatic purposes, he succeeded in hurting her, will he succeed again? he thought. On the short distance that Gogol and his guards had to walk to the border of the packaging company, they noticed many consumers wearing helmets giving them imaginary experiences, But these were, in fact, reenacted stories from ancient history, Helmet users seemed to be walking around the mall with a wide smile on their faces as they were not communicating with each other. Gogol shuddered at the sight of the people separated from each other by their helmets but made sure to remind himself to continue with his mission. The moment the guards removed the chip from his blood he started to remember the time he met Georgio thirty years ago in the ceremonial hall with the same group of children his age, his efforts were not in vain,

by the time Gogol ceased to daydream he was already on his way to Subara waiting for him in her isolated room. Subara rejoiced at the enormous change that is underway for her citizens, next to her sat Cisco, who for several days had stopped consuming transgenic food, which was evident on his face that became smoother by the day.

Gogol sat down and started to talk: "I come to you again peacefully, Georgio wants us to continue working together, you will give us supplies in return for rent without disputes."

Subara said: "You went straight to the point, last time you brought me a helmet it did me no good, I'm sure we can settle the disagreements between us, I'm just not sure how do you think we are damaging the white palace currently?"

Gogol continued: "For the sake of peace, I suggest that you stop the Exhibit that attracts migrants to the packaging company. For the sake of peace, I suggest purchasing from the food that you produce, I would love to go over the menu with you." Subara, however, was impressed by Cisco in regards to his human senses being sharpened, in particular, his sense of suspicion while he was whispering to Subara: "It seems to me that we have no interest in stopping the consumer attraction to our borders. We need more manpower now that we are all human."

240

Subara waved her hand contemptuously at Cisco and replied to Gogol: "I tend to agree with what you propose. I am really tired of the hostility between us. It's time for trade and flourishing."

Gogol answered: "If you're ready to give me a tour at your food production plant, we can start making the deal."

Chapter 43

Lenov tried in vain to reconnect to the advertising interface in the marketing department of the White Palace, he felt helpless. At the same time, Nikeo conducted an investigation and revealed to his surprise a new broadcast regarding the conversion of the "marketing wing" to the "worship wing". Nikeo read from the article: "Advertisements are automatically produced by the transmitted content from the helmets to the main computer. No manual production of advertisements will be required. From now the only active wing in the White Palace will engage in worship focused on Georgio." Rayban intervened, commenting: "That means our role as terrorists in the White Palace must change, too. Intelan, did you know any of this? Do you have any direction on how we can now violate the mental control of the palace?"

Intelan replied: "I had created a very substantial change to the helmets, a change that Georgio is unaware of."

"Please explain to us how the helmet works," Rayban instructed him in tone.

Intelan continued with the explanation: "Anyone carrying a chip in his body receives external information into the helmet he is wearing, such as historical stories and advertising

242

messages. The chip is originally used to transmit the information as a communication tool, but it has a dark use known only to those few who have an interest." Intelan smiled and paused for a moment, but the angry and impatient look of his partners at him kept him going: "The chip is used to filter out unwanted thoughts and memories that the regime does not like, it can be a childhood memory with content that Georgio does not want you to remember, that is why the deletion of the memory if it contains a forbidden to think details takes place. "

Rayban said: "that explains how I collapsed when I tried to condemn .."

Nike shouted: "Don't say his name!"

Rayban continued: "Apparently, there are supreme mental powers in our group if we were able to consciously rebel against the White Palace." Intelan replied: "The chip neutralizes memories and content but it cannot neutralize strong emotion against George ..."

Then he regretted and corrected: "The White Palace."

Intelan continued by revealing his secrets: "The helmet is designed to be an ultimate content maker and control tool in conjunction with the chip. It introduces you to a world of engaging content, giving Georgio exclusive control of the market. There is a function I added before I stopped serving Georgio Which allows a helmet user to recall his past rather than to be washed by the content. If there will be a slight change in the chip transmission and anyone using the helmet can be washed by the stream of deleted past memories as well as the information we will infuse. I have the honor to say that Georgio himself is not immune to a childhood memory while using the helmet ".

"So, all we have to do is to transfer forbidden information to helmet users," Lenov said. He felt that his senses are fading and his soul is filling with enthusiasm for the vast possibilities open to him: "If we run our own candidate for the prime minister position, we can inject the helmet users the idea of the importance of voting for him." Lenov laughed out loud, but the rest of the group fell silent.

Rayban said: "It's a great and legitimate idea, but how can we find a political candidate who will have the economic resources to run a campaign, Also where we will find someone that will agree to interview him and publish his idea's at the White Palace News Company."

Lenov and Nikeo answered together: "You will be this candidate!" The occupants of the room burst into contagious laughter, Ika was the last one to laugh after everyone relaxed.

Lenov said to Rayban: "No propaganda budget or news advertising is needed. While your candidacy is registered your campaign will be underground through the helmets."

Rayban replied: "We will still have to make a formal declaration of candidacy even though I do not understand why you think I am fit?"

Ika walked up to him and put her hand on his shoulder to Intelan's displeasure: "You are the only one to show leadership, your resistance group is among the few that exist in the big mall. If you can market yourself to the masses with the help of Intelan, I believe we can convince them that you are the most worthy candidate.".

Rayban began to show signs of consent and almost agreed to the idea proposed by Lenov. "We will need someone on the inside to help us get an interview with the White Palace News Company. Fortunately, I know someone like that."Rayban was talking about Mazda that ever since her disappointment from Sonny, she had left her job and a heartbroken layer of emptiness filled her room in the White Palace.

She looked at the helmet that lay on the nightstand beside her bed and thought, "I want to get away to other worlds for the rest of my life. I've already lost meaning in this world."

While lying down she got a call through the chip, in her mind she saw a call from a store that was listed as "closed for renovations", she knew it was Rayban. "Could he still be alive?" Mazda got up from her bed, took a long breath, and connected to a conversation with Rayban.

"I thought you were dead, I can't believe I'm talking to you again," Mazda said while a small tear popped under her left eye.

"We need your help Mazda, we need you to find us a news reporter who will agree to interview me as a competing prime ministerial candidate." She felt a breath of fresh air blowing near her when she heard Rayban's voice, and a memory of their short romance was awakened. Suddenly she stopped feeling lonely and a tiny smile came to her lips. Mazda thought about what Rayban said before answering: "I have access to the entire reporter's list. I will try to find the weak link for you."Rayban replied: "Because there is a fear of a blitz election and the elimination of one of the White Palace candidates, I ask that you come to us as soon as possible with the media representative."Rayban spoke to her in an authoritative and estranged voice but it didn't matter to Mazda, after the frustration that brought her back to the starting point she was glad to finally feel a part of something.

Before the end of the conversation, Rayban softened a bit and pleaded with her: "First of all, I want you to come over tomorrow morning. I have to see you again. We will go to the interview with the journalist." On that evening Mazda sent a message to all the journalists and production managers at the news company whose content is: "There is a suspected mole that jeopardizes the rule of law, freedom of the press, and the sanctity of Georgio's chair. If anyone has any information about journalists who are at risk please notify me in person, Guaranteed confidentiality! " Dozens of accusatory messages were sent to Mazda within minutes. The only one who didn't send a message was Sunan. "It is precisely the person who manages to NOT obey Georgio's orders was found worthy of being the journalist we can trust," Mazda thought.

Chapter 44

The meeting took many hours, Georgio delivered instructions and gave his teachings. Georgio felt uncomfortable, it was important to him to be with Gogol and Intelan and they were not present to advise him and direct him about his vision. Georgio saw himself as a visionary that his henchmen were supposed to exercise his orders. "No problem," he thought to himself. "I will implement all the goals I have set out in my ingenious mind and pass it directly to the foremen." Georgio came out of the conference room first, leaving the managers utterly speechless. He sat down in front of his work console which was relatively modest and intimate to a regular work console.

First, he contacted the professor of history Britnick: "You thought you could get away with it? I need more historical materials so I can launch it into the helmets of the users, right now I Am the graphics and content department," Georgio laughed out loud.

Britnick couldn't help to recognize His Highness who contacted him: "I wired you a legal historical content, Your Holiness, would you like me to edit more content? What time are you interested in? Ancient Greece? Japan's Meiji era? British colonization of Australia I have fascinating topics... ".

Georgio answered him firmly and impatiently: "It seems to me that you are wasting valuable time in order not to be fired by me. Know that your time is running short, you must transfer all your historical materials so that I can make them into dreams items for my helmets, and then you will resign or else I will make you retire. . " Professor Britnik recognized this ominous voice from the voice of many kings from all the history book he had read.

Immediately he sent Georgio a large file and replied in a frightening and stuttering voice: "I will make a tremendous effort to complete the rest of the historical scripts for you as soon as possible..." Georgio loved this kind of tone so he terminated the conversation with the professor. Because the content and advertising department was closed, Georgio had to take the professor's big file and send it for easy processing on the main computer that was the last to serve Georgio. From there, thousands of historical stories were sent to the helmets of all users whose ads were hidden in their content to encourage purchase. Georgio took another share of the means of production and control. Intelan's idea to create a virtual currency to be used instead of the government currency was unnecessary, as he would still rule the government with the help of his new P.M Renault or the good old Peugeot. The key challenge remaining on Georgio's agenda was to ensure the independence of the Big mall versus the packaging company that supplied raw materials that the mall state had to pay for. To that end, he sent Gogol on a suicide mission. The last step into total dominance was to upgrade his nanobots, for that he contacted Professor Pfizera: "I am still working on biological nanobots that will survive under external environmental conditions."

Georgio replied: "Your schedule is getting shorter, my mechanical nanobots as well as Subara's nanobots, my competitor, can carry any outer resource but are not resistant to the outside conditions over time. I require that the nanobots will be able to survive outside and be as powerful as the mechanical ones."

The professor replied: "In my theory, biological nanobots with photosynthetic capabilities will be able to do whatever your mechanical nanobots do only with the ability to survive a very long time outside and conserve their energy inside the mall."

Georgio was impatient, throwing another threat into the chip in her body: "I'm ready to give you any amount of resource or funds to complete your research as quickly as possible, but if you don't finish your work in the next few weeks..." Georgio abruptly cut off the conversation with the professor and went to bed in his luxurious bed while Heinze sleeping in a separate room with his baby.

250

The next day he was ready for the fateful meeting with Manpowerena, the human resources director, she was mentally drained of all the layoff calls she had to make with most of the managers of the big mall. "Sit down, please, when you're ready we'll discuss all the unnecessary departments to shut down," Georgio told her as he sat in front of his console, ignoring the bleak Manpowerena. She went over with him about the closing of the copywriting department, on the advertising and marketing department, the food pills manufacturing department that also automatically worked on Georgio's direct instruction via the nanobots. "The hovercraft that brought raw materials to the White Palace operated on behalf of the packaging company. All the maintenance, entertainment, and nightlife of the White Palace can also be terminated. In fact, what remains is to close the news company, after all the mall's consumers are becoming addicted users of the helmets so we have no one to broadcast to".

Georgio continued: "Right now the mall security company can be closed. I don't see any cyber-terrorism or physical danger that threatens me when my activity is directly monitored by me. Did you do what I asked you to do?"

Manpowerna shook her head positively, adding: "I recruited a security manager who used to be a junior seller in one of your stores. Her job was to catch hackers on the intranet but so far I haven't heard from her."

Georgio nodded with satisfaction and replied: "Due to the futility of the security department and the lack of professionalism of its head, I am forced to close this department. Give the manager and the employees their dismissal, accompanied by a report detailing this." Manpowerena nodded: I am sure the dismissal would seem justified, thus prevent an uprising. "

Georgio laughed: "Better still, make sure a reporter for the news company will write an article about the failing manager of the security company, that will create a positive public opinion towards the layoffs."

Manpowerna dared to burst into Georgio's words: "But why does an omnipotent person like you need all of these manipulations? Why not just say that you want to fire them just because you are entitled to?" Georgio answered her as he left the room: "Manipulation is what's making it so much fun and pleasurable."

Chapter 45

Mazda sat down in the train cart on her way to the southern part of the big mall. She made an appointment with Sunan in the White Palace newsroom studio, but first, she had to pick up Rayban. Mazda lusted to meet Rayban, which sparked a flame of emotions. She looked at the window through which the landscape was blurred, recalling the moments of making love with Rayban, a love she had once hoped would be fulfilled with Sony. Minute by minute she internalized the fact that Sony is just a great, glamorous reflection of a real, private, and different person. Meanwhile, in the hidden shop, Intelan tried to program Rayban's message to broadcast to anyone wearing the helmet: "I need you to stand up authoritatively and tell everyone you meet there that you are the prime ministerial candidate who was chosen to rescue them from their severe addiction." Intelan turned to Rayban, who shook his head, and after a short concern he had in his mind about what he would do, he asked Lenov to put the helmet on Rayban's head and activate it while Rayban was lying on his armchair.

As soon as he closed his eyes in reality, he discovered in front of his eyes huge stone walls, around which a vast desert and numerous camels surrounded him. Two spear-armed guards with dark skin guarded the gate. Rayban addressed them: "I am the prime ministerial candidate, I promise to rescue you from your addiction." Two guards bowed and opened the gate that was a few meters high. Rayban entered the walled city, surrounded by the scents of spices he had first in his life felt in his nose, passing through a market full of fruits and vegetables and all kinds of exotic dishes. While walking around he was surrounded entirely by gaudy hawks and bargaining shoppers and encountered sheep and chickens running around him. Then he continued walking through narrow alleys and streets until he encountered a beggar asking for a handout. He reached into his own pocket and found no coin, just a written scroll. To the beggar, he said the same sentence he told the guards, the beggar in return indicated with his finger where he should go. Beyond the corner stands a magnificent round-arched palace. Rayban's way to the palace was easy, no one stood in his way, the palace gate was also open. Over the pools and baths, he saw women washing their feet, dressed modestly in antique dresses. Rayban entered the main hall where the king was sitting, who impressed Rayban with his expression on his face. The king's body was covered in golden and red silk robes and a sparkling beaded crown on his head. The counselor standing next to the king waved his hand down, he instinctively understood that he should bow and so he did. The consultant picked up a stone tablet on which many marks were engraved and began to read aloud:

* "I am Cyrus, king of Babylon, the great king, the fierce king, the king of Babylon, the king of shomer and Akkad ... Ashbarel and Nebo love his reign and who want to rejoice in their government... My vast armies walked peacefully in Babylon... I am worried about the peace of Babylon and the other holy cities. I court the gods sitting within them, and made them a worldly sanctuary. I convened all their inhabitants and resumed their residence. "*

Rayban believed that he had come to another world that seemed real to him, he turned to the king with his head raised to him: "Please release the residents of the Big mall to the Promised Land, you can be our Prime Minister if you just let us worship our God."Rayban did not understand where this text was planted in his mind, but he took the scroll out of his pocket and rolled it, and saw the same text written in it. The king's counselor came to him, took the scroll from him, and brought it to the king. Suddenly, Rayban woke up from the dream he was in and remember saying, "I am your alternate prime ministerial candidate, I promise to free you from the addiction you have." King Cyrus was furious and ordered his guards to catch Rayban, as soon as a spear lodged in his stomach, he immediately awoke, dripping with cold sweat as his heart pounded rapidly and his body clasped in Lenov's arms. Intelan smiled and said calmly: "I think this recording of yours will be sufficient for us. I'll make sure this show is shown to anyone who uses helmets. Apparently, Mazda arrived at the group's whereabouts and watched Rayban's foggy facial expression while dreaming in his helmet's fantasy. After a short time he took for the sack of recovery, Rayban wore an elegant Hologramic suit, accompanied by Mazda, they came out holding hands toward the nearest train station leading to the White Palace: "I've never officially and legally entered the White Palace. It's always been in a hidden way." Mazda smiled at him and said: "I am happy to see you, I hope that interview at the White Palace will go smoothly." They spent the rest of the trip holding hands while looking at each other. When they reached the entrance of the White Palace, Sunan emerged from behind one of the guards at the entrance:

"I will pay the 100 eular that are needed for the entry."

Mazda replied: "I have arranged for you an exclusive interview. I trust you will be fair." Sunan smiled and the three of them continued toward the newsroom offices. As the Central Edition broadcast began, Mazda sat backstage while the edition's hologram-panoramic shot showed the host and Sunan sitting across from Rayban.

The host started by saying: "Tonight we will present to you a new independent candidate who wants to be elected as the Prime Minister." The host turned to Sunan: "Sunan, I wanted to know how you get to him?" The host's words seemed to have been dictated in advance. Sunan replied: "This is one of the senior White Palace wingers who has drawn my attention to another independent candidate, except for Renault, who is already known as the inspirational candidate in the big mall that challenges Georgio's rule."

The host turned to Rayban: "So how different are you from Renault who has already promised to be a comprehensive reformer of the administration against the White Palace."

Rayban was preparing to respond firmly to how he intends to fight the addiction of the big mall consumers who use helmets and also to impose heavy taxes on Georgio's Democratic Allies companies, but then the interviewer interrupted and turned to Mazda: "I want to call the information security chief at the White Palace, due to severe deficiencies regarding the security of the palace, a high order was issued to fire all the security personnel of the White Palace, is that correct? " A member of the production team pushed Mazda forcefully towards Rayban, Mazda found herself exposed to the host's question. Sunan was surprised that during the broadcast, the production man pushed Mazda in front of the camera.

Mazda, who was totally astonished due to her exposure, replied: "I had no idea we were fired. I have held my fiduciary duties so far." The interviewer pointed out firmly to

Mazda: "I know it looks like a live layoff, but according to the source of the big mall's personnel department you actually got this job even though you don't have any management skills and experience in the field of security, is that the truth?

Mazda stammered while standing next to Rayban: "You better turn the question over to those who recruited me for the job. I was indeed just a saleswoman at a helmet store ..."

The interviewer interrupted the broadcast in front of Rayban and Mazda: "So it turns out that there is a strong justification for the mass dismissal in the White Palace, the recruitment of incompetent people that caused a severe failure of the palace departments. We may encounter further failures that will result in layoffs in more departments." The broadcast went on to other stories and the host ignored Sunan, Rayban, and Mazda that the camera had already lost focus from them. One of the mall guards accompanied Rayban and Mazda who found themselves outside the walls of the White Palace.

* The Cyrus Cylinder Cyrus Statement

Chapter 46

In the corridors of the packaging company, a rumor is spreading about various strange deaths that are occasionally happening to the company's employees. There have been no rumors in the packaging company for many years, all news was reported to the chief executive of the "general affairs", the manager used to convene a Blitz committee whose task was to confirm the publication of the news items in the official announcements and in the general newspaper of the packaging company. The hybrids found no interest in gossiping and spreading rumors and any information that came to their ears from the newspaper or the Announcer (depending on the length of the news) was accepted by them as a fact. It was impossible to ignore the connection between the transformation of the packaging company's employees into whole people, and the difference in the taste of food in its composition and texture. All company employees felt their skin becomes smoother or their excess hair disappearing. The bee people initially felt intense pains in the chest and pelvis that became less rigid, but mainly in the reluctance to work and, on the other hand, more willing to connect, talk and consolidate. There were mass crowds and the day-to-day rumors revolved around the people who died suddenly. This proclamation bypassed this committee every day until the masses of people gathered under charismatic workers' leaders who agitated the crowd to demand information about the horrific deaths.

One day, Subara looked out of her office window on the top floor of a building that scratched the glass dome and saw a huge crowd screaming their lungs out:

"We want a solution! Fight the plague for us!"

And even more alarming calls:

"No life, no work! Don't work until you get well!" etc.

Cisco stood behind Subara as he wrapped her pelvis in his arms that had weakened since he stopped being a hybrid, a man-pitbull, Cisco's soft touch was very pleasing to Subara's skin. She was disturbed by Gogol's stay in her office, but he refused to leave his room every time with another excuse. Gogol remained in her office because he hoped to be able to remember in a particular manner some details from his childhood, now that he's temporarily disconnected from the chip's control. One day during a meeting with Subara, he recalled that she was the first to use the prototype of the helmet he gave her. He dared to stop the meeting and ask her for the helmet to help him fall asleep at night. Subara answered him with diplomatic courtesy. Gogol realized that this was his last chance, and went to his room with the helmet, he wanted to escape from the feeling of loneliness that was bothering him since separating from his beloved wife. There was a yearning for a warm family that he never knew. This impulse was stronger than any biological or political survival tool and so he was willing to risk using this method. He was wearing the helmet while lying in his bed without anyone seeing him.

Outside the palace, one of the former owl men, the head of the Researchers Chamber, was responsible for the quality of the food in the company. He cried out most directly the results of the latest test findings without giving the masses any technical details: "Our food has been poisoned, the food composition is different, not only is it preventing us from being hybrid, but it is also killing us!" At that moment there was a roar of shouting from several people in the crowd, most of the people in the crowd left in shock. "Could the Queen have secretly poisoned us instead of turning us back into a human form?" That was the thought of almost every man with common sense. Then a frantic onslaught of the crowds began on the gates of the royal building which was nothing more than a gray concrete structure with dull and ornate geometric shapes. The crowd was barely pushed through the narrow gate that was the only passage to the tower except for the high concrete walls that surrounded it. Subara was leaving the throne room, walked to the balcony, thinking of a way to get out of her seat despite the terror she felt.

Gogol found himself wandering half-naked in moist rain forest thickets, he really felt naked with a real piece of cloth covering his pubic and another half piece of cloth surrounding one breast and extending over his shoulder. Despite the strange feeling, he continued to walk toward the scent of smoke that gently curled around the tree branches. Gogol ran into the thicket of smoke as he smelled the stifling odor growing stronger until he reached a clearing in the woods and in it some log cabins. The smell of smoke seemed to come from a large bonfire around which sat a happy bunch of people playing musical instruments that produced natural sounds in a simple melody. Gogol was accustomed only to complex electronic sounds, it was a refreshing innovation for him to come closer and see a woman rattle with rhymes, another man playing a string instrument for most of the melody while a second man sat beside them next to the bonfire hitting on a leather drum. The sea of smiles directed at him as he walked closer to the group who was greatly amazed him, a smiling woman who was twice his height approached him to his dismay. She raised him as if he were a small pet: "My son, where did you run? You could fall victim to a wild beast or one of the hunters from the big dome." Gogol turned his head and saw beyond the treetops the moon shining on a huge glass dome, at that moment he did not realize that he was part of a dream and did not know the dome is actually the big mall from which he came from. What Gogol expected to find forgotten at that moment, he forgot the true reality that included his coming-of-age story from the moment Georgio found him to the last moment subara's helmet was placed on his head. Gogol perceived reality as a little boy holding onto his mother, yet in those moments he still could not break away from the illusion of the helmet in his consciousness.

Subara and Cisco hugged each other tightly. Suddenly, their office door had been completely breached by the crowd that was attacking Subara as Cisco fled. He jumped on the porch rail that led him safely to the roof of the tower. Subara did not survive the harsh blows incurred by the whole-humans. Two bodies were placed side by side on the floor, one was of Subara's bleeding body and the other was of Gogol's body whose consciousness existed in a different reality.

Chapter 47

Fox waited next to Renault's sleeping capsule, but the interviewee Renault and his colleague Sunan didn't to came. A few weeks later, when it was time for the main propaganda broadcast to focus on the final confrontation between the three candidates, Sunan got a message from Georgio himself: "Why wasn't Renault interviewed?"

Sunan was startled for a moment, the message also received by Fox: "Why didn't we interview Renault? Why did you get the third and unofficial candidate for an interview?"

Sunan replied to Fox with a message through the chip: "I stopped believing in Georgio's candidates ..." Sunan stopped by herself from saying the explicit name and completed the sentence: "The White Palace... in my opinion, you can interview Renault yourself." Fox who was torn at that moment between his love for Sunan and his loyalty and fear of disobeying Georgio preferred to break away from the conversation, but his heart had been broken because of this rift. He knew he had lost Sunan who had not returned love to him. Sunan went on to prepare for the main broadcast, the scoop was a surprising combination of Rayban broadcasting with Peugeot and Renault, with Rayban confronting them and raising stiff issues that are not allowed to be mentioned. Sunan received an anonymous text message:

"You will still regret what you did."

Former religious priests who had a sacred career in the palace went on the air. They raised their concerns with the candidates about the lack of employment and budget allocated to religious affairs to the "United Democratic companies" in the White Palace. This budget did not fund career-clergy officials, as there were almost no workers in the White Palace except for the media and some soldiers guarding the palace. Because the broadcast was made in the desolate rink of the White Palace, the aim was to fill the compound with a crowd to look as though it was full despite the complaints of the newly fired people. Renault promised the fired people to allocate a special budget to directly employ them outside the White Palace. This proposal caused outrageous reactions in the consumer audience, how the religion could take place outside the Holy White Palace: "A sacred career must not be conducted in an area of consumerism and idleness." This is how the consumer representative who was brought up for discussion with his family argued. His wife and children seemed to marvel at the beauty of the palace and the magnificent apartments that used to house the palace workers' families there.

Another consumer representative asked: "What will the immigrants who have just returned from the packaging company following the revolution that went on there? Will they be eligible for a universal minimum salary?"

Peugeot, the conservative, replied: "Anyone who carries a chip in his body and returns to the big mall is entitled to a universal minimum wage so that he can act as a beneficial consumer."

A bunch of returning migrants applauded Peugeot and one of their representatives stood up and said: "When will we get full meals that are not nutritional pills? Why don't you open delicious tangible food restaurants?"

Renault answered the question: "I promise I will make a reform and I will personally ask Georgio to open a new food chain. I'm sure his holiness will be convinced."

The immigrant representative continued to ask: "What about employment? What about a consumer who wants to integrate with more activities?" The delegate refrained from saying the sacred words, work or career, and used the word activity so he will not antagonize the people who hear him, already there were cheers from the audience: "Why only nanobots can do craft activities? We also want to help the nanobots!" Sunan felt that the audience was not prepared for the blatant things that Rayban intended to say but nonetheless turned to the broadcast host who was sitting next to her:

"Madam, with your permission, I would like to add the third candidate to the broadcast." Sunan did not understand from where did she get the mental powers that enabled her to do so such a courageous, unacceptable, and contradictory act.

Rayban burst into the broadcast in his voice without revealing his face: "If I may, I will answer some of the audience questions"

The host scolded him: "Of course, you are not allowed to do that!"

But then Peugeot burst into her words with a smile: "Let him say his words, of course, no one would agree with such an extreme person and it would be better if we would respect his right to speak if we wanted to respect democracy."

Rayban went on and said, "I think the nanobots should serve all of the people, but also, every consumer should be allowed to participate in a creative work or initiative."

One of the White Palace ex-workers burst into anger, saying, "How do you allow anyone to make a sacred career?" People like you despise Georgio's name and palace. Only the mall owner can decide who is allowed to work. "

Rayban tried to wrestle with the scorn that came from the crowd: "People have no freedom to work, only the white palace-controlled nanobots."

Rayban knew that every word he uttered would send his voice through the chip in his body and eventually could hit him back like a boomerang. He picked his words carefully.

Renault saw how Rayban stole the rebel's role against him: "Because of you, the packaging company will bring us to our collapse. We must not change the rules. We need a responsible leader to reform the mall state."Rayban tried to interrupt his words but when he tried to say the word "Georgio" he felt dizzy and kept quiet. Luckily Mazda was at his side in the hidden shop and served him a glass of water before he passed out.

Sunan summed up Rayban's remarks: "So there seems to be someone who wants to propose a more radical reform, and it's good to give him a chance." The host whispered: "I'm afraid this time you are exaggerating." Immediately, Sunan was blinded and her entire body was also glowing as golden berries that wrapped her were coming down on her, three feet above her head. It was a cluster of nanobots that turned her body into an enlightened mass that took off into the sky in front of the raging crowd. It was unclear to them why this was being done, but to channel the panic that arose in the audience for positive vibes, the host ordered to end the news broadcast and called the crowd to pray for Georgio's unlimited power. The nanobots accumulated by Georgio were sent to Sunan and lifted her up through the packaging company ceiling out of the Big mall, they continued along the desert for only a few meters but the sun and heavy humidity did not allow them to continue beyond that and they dropped Sunan on the soft sand as her big eyes poured tears. She realized that she had been brutally exiled in addition to losing her job at the news company. Luckily the mall gate remains open. She did not want to stay in the desert under the blazing sun that was foreign to her, choosing to return to an unknown future in the mall.

Chapter 48

Since the mysterious coup in the packaging company, the reinforcements of guardians from the mall state have been posted to oversee the passage of the people to the big mall. Anarchy caused unemployment and disorganization in the packaging company, a lack of order made the former company workers want to cross the border into a legendary lifestyle, after the collapse of obedience and with the supervisory chain enforced by the foremen. The curiosity that sprang to their hearts, lust, and human greed led the crowd to flock to the entrance of the big mall. Those who were allowed to relocate, or more accurately, were the returning consumers, who had been immersed in a culture of artistic performances, improvised historical museums, and musical instruments of all times. The cultured consumers were able to understand that change was needed, but the candidate that attracted the most attention was Renault that Georgio delights to honor. The mall prime minister's election day had been held for the first time in the year 5 AO (counting the mall's opening). Historically, it was opened as a shelter for the climate change survivors and then sold by a bankrupt banker to Georgio's great-grandfather. The first elections were held under the supervision and watchful eye of Georgio's great-grandfather and this tradition continued to the good fortune of Rayban and his partners in the plot. Ika watched the strange lines of code and the holograms that were painted in the air by her partner Intelan, She knew he was doing something incredibly important that was beyond everyone's Intellectual understanding, waving like a Philharmonic Orchestra conductor, evading the security firewalls of the mall's intranet he made all the helmet users at the big mall see the message in their minds.

For the first time in his sacred career, Fox was chosen to broadcast as the chief reporter just a few feet from the ballot box: It seems like all the voters are the proud owners of a helmet "Fox chuckled in front of the camera broadcasting the live photos to those watching the broadcast through the chip they had to carry in their bodies. Fox interviewed a family whose little boy's addiction was so severe that his mother had to pull his face out of his helmet for all the viewers of the broadcast to see his cute face. As soon as they removed his helmet, he asked his mother to take him to the virtual liquor pub to take a sip out of the intoxicating alcoholic beverage he saw in the commercial, but his mother firmly silenced him.

Fox asked the father of the family: "May I ask who you want to vote for?"

The father of the family said with a face full of fear: "either Renault or Peugeot or ..." and continued towards the ballot box with his wife while their children trotting after them. The name Rayban, echoed loudly in their heads until they reached the election console, and left them with no choice but the explicit name Rayban. They immediately left as they rushed to put on their helmets as the addictive urge was even more powerful than the fear of exposing their choice. Fox approached a stern middle-aged man whose hair was graying and was wearing a holographic shimmering cloak and was helmet-free.

Fox asked him: "You don't seem to have the privilege to use a helmet, sir. Can I ask you who did you choose for the next term?"

The stern man proudly said: "I'll vote for Peugeot, he'll keep things like they used to be, I remember once I was talking to people through a chip or face to face today they're immersed in their imaginary world, all because of those helmets ..." The man kept walking and Fox Didn't bother to chase him. A young couple caught his eye, He instantly recognize that they came from the packaging company according to the physical worker's clothes they were wearing, he quickly said:

"You look like a poor packaging company worker."

The woman chuckled: "Why do you think I am poor? The cut of the suit doesn't suit me?" The lightweight blue synthetic garment did indeed complement her shapely body to the delight of her partner who put his hand on her shoulder.

Fox smiled and asked the man: "I hear by the dialect that you are the consumers of the mall, why did you come back from the packaging company, and what is your impression of this awful place?"

The man replied: "It was very interesting to travel there, they invested heavily in the representation of the pre-mall era. It is a pity they do not understand that Georgio forbids thinking about the pre-big mall era that caused all the destruction in the world." The man knew he was being taped and so he did not want to talk about the pleasant artistic and musical experience he absorbed there.

Instead, he was quick to finish the interview and said, "We're in a hurry to vote."

Fox asked as they walked away: "Who do you plan to vote for?"

And the man shouted: "Don't know yet, either Renault or the other candidate." Which revealed his rather awkward position that made Fox laugh.

Fox continued to broadcast to the main news studio as they counted the votes. Rayban and Mazda watched the broadcast through the chip in their minds. They both sat shaking and stressed, hands crossed, only Ika and Intelan were calm and rest assured. Ika, who has long been influenced by eating the mall's food pills, has become an almost complete, heavy, but handsome human girl, one of whom has been holding Intelan's hand. Lenov and Nikeo were disbelieving until the broadcast host read the results:

"Peugeot-23%, Renault-19%, Rayban-58%."

There was radio silence in the studio, an immediate dismissal notice was sent from Manpowerna to all newsroom employees. Nevertheless, business continued as usual. The host paused for a moment and went on to say: "This is the end of the broadcast. Rayban is the prime minister, probably a technical glitch. We will check the results and will keep you updated." The old managing console is designed so that the prime minister's room opens to the elected prime minister use only! Rayban did not know how his control would be obtained, but he knew that he had little time to implement the reforms, he would have to confront Georgio to secure his place, luckily he had Mazda and his friends to consult with. Rayban did not have the option of broadcasting through the chip but had the police and the big mall's management console. He stood up and said bravely: "I'm going to the government building to make a victory speech, who's coming with me?" All of his friends went after him without exception. All the residents of the mall received messages into their chip against the elected Rayban, including the mall state police who were too confused to keep the order and did not prevent Rayban and his entourage from entering the government building. Mazda told Rayban who sat on the prime minister's throne in his tiny room: "I will help you to take the throne, it is clearly a case of doing or die!." Mazda knew that defeat meant death.

Chapter 49

Mazda was accompanied by Coca to the main archive. Coca, the current government representative and secretary of prime minister Peugeot, ordered to inaugurate Mazda as her replacement in the new government auditor's office. Mazda was allowed to enter the archive room now that the police were under Rayban's control. Coca was unaware of Mazda's plot that was made as a masterwork by Intelan, she breathed a sigh of relief as they both entered the large archive room. This time, Mazda was able to glean important functions with which the nanobots activate and deactivate the chips. Mazda acted according to the instructions she received from above, she didn't need any authority or knowledge. The courage she displayed throughout her life was very useful at that moment. Coca condescendingly remarked: "young lady, why are you rummaging through those folders? Come and see what's relevant to you. "Coca knew she would soon lose her job and be thrown into Peugeot's arms on his next job at the White Palace. Mazda ignored her and concentrated on searching for the interface to which she could connect the memory card that was given to her. She found the required function and immediately transferred it to the card that Intelan gave her, everything went smoothly without any suspicion. Mazda did not believe she had reached the final stage of her plan, a meeting with Professor Pfizera, but first, she had to shake off

Coca. All the security workers and computer technicians who supervised the nanobots that created the chips and many other products had already been fired by Georgio, Mazda slipped into an empty hallway and ran in the opposite direction to Coca's slow, indifferent walk.

"You won't be able to avoid me for much longer. I know you took something from the archive. I don't need anyone to catch you," the voice echoed in her head.

Mazda reached the faculty offices in a rush of forces from where she entered Pfizera's lab. The scientist looked at her exhausted hand: "Who are you my child and why do you look so scared?"

Mazda responded: "As the elected government's quality controller, I ask that you provide me with the prototype of the nanobots you have developed..."

The professor replied in astonishment: "Miss, what are you talking about? I just finished developing the first prototype of photosynthetic biological nanobots. There is a culture in this petri dish that provides an endless amount of surviving nanobots outside the mall."

Mazda handed the professor her card and asked: "All I was told was that you should load these nanobots with this code.

The professor who was only motivated by her scientific curiosity load the card into her computer console for a few minutes and seemed to be trying to couple it with her nanobots. Mazda didn't understand what she waiting for but as the green light nanobots began to fly across the room she raised her head in admiration and heard the professor: "This is an ultimate combination of my invention and your code, the nanobots will now work in a decentralized way with anyone who will communicate with them, independently, unmediated by any server. Really! a genius code you've developed. "

Mazda laughed at the lights: "I really didn't create this code, this implementation was developed by who was the head of the Computing Department at the White Palace."

The professor jumped out of her chair: "Look at how the software spreads them out of the room. The code seems to be instructing them to manipulate any chip they encounter."

Mazda asked her in amazement: "So does that mean Georgio is going to take over them too?"

The professor grabbed Mazda enthusiastically: "No! That means I got into serious trouble with Georgio the Great. I was supposed to hand him the new nanobots, but now they have a life of their own and they fly everywhere as your eyes can see, without the control of the main computer! " Mazda and the professor were the first to alter their chip, the professor changed to a coat hologram and went out the door: "I am going to disappear, I see that my chip has been cut off from the mainframe which means I can escape without His Holiness knowing where I am." Mazda herself stopped hearing the reverberating voices in her head and realized that Intelan had caused Professor Pfaizera's biological nanobots to bypass the chip's control. Mazda was about to leave the White Palace, unfortunately, the academy was on the second floor of the main tower in the palace. She anxiously entered the elevator and pressed down to get to the ground floor. Then, to her surprise, the elevator went upstairs without Mazda controlling its operation. The elevator door opened and at the entrance stood Georgio, the same middle-aged old man with a mustache and a chip with which he controlled his main server and his nanobots. He approached the frightened Mazda standing inside the elevator until she screamed in horror, she knew exactly who he was! Georgio clung to her and yelled into her ear: "You will pay for it dearly!" Mazda was dazzled by the power of the nanobots accumulating in yellow, electric light as strong currents pounding all over her body. She lost control of her limbs, all she could see was a white light. Mazda lost consciousness and fainted. The elevator door closed and after a few minutes, Heinze opened it again, carrying the baby with one hand. She tried to wake her up with her left hand but in vain. Heinze picked her up with one hand as the baby in her other hand and with her last ounce of strength pressed the button that took them to the ground floor of the White Palace tower. She dragged Mazda in her left hand as the baby cried in her right hand, the white palace was completely desolate, only green glitter glistening in the glass dome that hid the white sunlight. This time Mazda was riding while unconscious on the train car until she reached the last stop, the government building. Heinze asked to get the poor miss some medical help, she knew that medical treatment would not come from Georgio and his nanobots. She went out with the baby and disappeared across the alleyways of the big mall. Mazda remained unconscious for a full hour at the station next to the government building until one of the police officers have reached her and carried her to Rayban's office. Rayban kissed his darling lover and put her to sleep on the couch in his office. He knelt down and whispered in her ear: "You're a heroine, you risked yourself for everyone. I will order the cops who are already been disconnected from the old chip to stop implanting old chips in people's bodies."

Chapter 50

A flood of people began to flow from the packaging company into the big mall from the moment Rayban gave the order. Any immigrant who came to the mall state could choose whether or not a chip would be implanted in him, of course, everyone agreed to have the chip implanted in them so they could communicate with each other and the authorities. The breaking news release was broadcast by the announcer and also in writing: "Here is the first broadcast of the: " Free News Company" and here is the news from the big mall: The new Prime Minister decided that from now on his holiness Georgio will be a symbolic religious figure who has no authority and can not intervene on business matters. Georgio will not own the big mall. And in another matter... "The announcer added:" A new law faculty will be open at the White Palace Academy, graduates may be employed by consumers for the first time. " The announcer went on to report on the many reforms that Rayban initiated, including Georgio being cut off from his control over the means of production: the nanobots and communication: the chip. Rayban decided not to hurt Georgio and not to take revenge for the serious injury he caused to his beloved Mazda. Rayban sat next to Mazda's bed and talked to his friends Nikeo and Lenov who were sitting next to him, one has been appointed to the position of the Interior Minister and the other held the position of the Minister of Economy and Communications respectively.

"I'm glad you guys came up with the idea of keeping Georgio alive, It is so tempting to take revenge on him, "Rayban said in a jarring tone and grinding teeth.

Since his childhood, Lenov, who was Rayban's psychic support replied: "Just know that the greatest revenge on a man like Georgio is to make his loss his power, the suffering he felt when he was isolated and depleted of his ability to control is even more terrible than death for him." Nikeo smiled and giggled as if he did not understand the deep meaning of what he just heard, but this trio had known each other for years and respected each other the way they did without judging.

Intelan who was appointed Minister of Science and Technology understood Rayban's move, he too had thought of vengeance on Georgio but understood in his cold and analytical thinking that a living Georgio will keep the stability.

"I decided to move on and I will try to develop a technology that would quickly allow building residential buildings for the people of the mall state." Intelan smiled excitedly, Ika, who was appointed chief of the mall state Police

Headquarters, held Intelan's hand as they walked through the shops and replied: "Darling, it's nice that you moved on despite what you went through." She put a kiss on his cheek, "There is such a bright future ahead of us, why should we concentrate on revenge? This place requires great creativity and new inventions!" Intelan said as his heart was filled with love, not only for Ika but for all the consumers and new packaging company residents who came together. Georgio was locked in his room, he looked through the glass which gave him a panoramic view of the Big mall. His mind was empty and he sat depressed and bored by the fact that his main server could manage nothing for him now that the old nanobots were inferior to the new nanobots in their numbers and abilities. From being a ruler he became an abusive terrorist and decided to disable his nanobots from any activity. Georgio spent his time watching the endless content of delusions recorded from all helmet users, it was a long and varied film that would keep him busy for the rest of his life. Gogol, on the other hand, decided to wake up from the hallucination that had enveloped him long after the food supply at his bed had run out. Hunger bothered him and pushed him to get up and disengage from the helmet. The light of the room dazzled his eyes and the smell of intense decay surrounded the room. His senses awoke and stunned him until he almost passed out, he could barely walk due to his degenerate muscles and his empty stomach. Only when he saw Subara's decaying body did he prefer to have his two legs move him as quickly as possible out of the structure he had spent many days in. After recovering, he discovered the packaging company was almost depleted of its residents, except for the nostalgia enthusiasts and single-minded people, the few who still remained there without action. He tried to contact his wife and succeeded: "I do not know what your situation is now but I decided to try to find my family. They are outside the mall dome."

She replied to him: "Just now that I was looking for you, I miss you, dear husband, I no longer use a helmet, no one uses them anymore."

Gogol replied: "It's not about you my beloved, it's about my decision to try to connect the dots between my forgotten past that was taken from me, it's something I owe to myself. I have to check the veracity of my family's existence."

Adoba nodded: "I'll miss you, I know you won't come back because it's dangerous out there." She burst into bitter tears but knew she had nothing to do with him anymore, her husband Gogol was a man of rigid deeds and decisions, one who was very good at convincing than being convinced.

Gogol finish the call and continued on his way out of the only mall that was the big mall from the packaging company area toward the sand dunes with a small vehicle capable of levitation. He knew the vehicle would not serve him for the entire trip and that he might fail in his mission to find a sign of life, but something pulled him to drive away from the only place he had ever known.

Mazda who was completely detached from the chip in her body, while wearing a helmet she daydreamed that she was in the packaging company. And here she was, a really small girl, she found herself leaving her house for another day at school. She came to the room where her father, mother, and two little brothers lived, the whole family used to eat in the packaging company dining room with the rest of their kind. She remembered her father's warm embrace and the kiss of her mother throughout the walk to the dining room. All of these sights have been seen by Intelan, Rayban, and their other friends by a hologram presentation screened at the Prime Minister's Office. Intelan attached a helmet to the hologram display that projected Mazda's dreams and thus everyone experienced her memories with her, which she produced in her mind during her coma.
Intelan tried to reassure Rayban: "I hope she gets out of the coma soon."
Rayban replied: "Me too, I already miss her, meanwhile she's dreaming."
Intelan replied: "It's not a dream, my friend. She remembers her magical childhood.

The end

Made in the USA
Monee, IL
07 July 2026